A
Harlequin
Romance

OTHER

Harlequin Romances

by SUE PETERS

WHEELS
OF CONFLICT

by

SUE PETERS

HARLEQUIN BOOKS   TORONTO
WINNIPEG

Harlequin edition published October 1975
SBN 373-01916-5

Original hard cover edition published in 1975
by Mills & Boon Limited.

All the characters in this book have no existence outside the
imagination of the Author, and have no relation whatsoever to
anyone bearing the same name or names. They are not even
distantly inspired by any individual known or unknown to the
Author, and all the incidents are pure invention

The Harlequin trade mark, consisting of the word
HARLEQUIN and the portrayal of a Harlequin, is registered
in the United States Patent Office and in the Canada Trade
Marks Office.

Printed in Canada

1916

CHAPTER ONE

'SIGN here, please, miss.'

Sherry took the book from the counter clerk, signed her name with a flourish, and grasped the errant piece of luggage firmly by the handle.

What a lot of money the air terminals must waste every year, reuniting passengers with their mislaid baggage, she marvelled, mentally calculating what her own trip out from Beacon Downs would cost the airline, and multiplying it by the frequent repetitions she made every holiday season for the same purpose. Even now, near to Christmas, and with the passenger flow reduced from the summer months, the airport still had to use their services for this purpose at least twice every week. 'Not that I should complain,' she told herself hastily. Other people's forgetfulness brought business to Manders Motors, and her uncle's fleet of large, steel-grey private hire cars, of which she was now temporarily in charge.

She swung the suitcase off the desk, relieved to find that it was not too heavy, and pushed through the double glass doors into the passenger lounge.

'Another hour,' she thought thankfully, 'and I can get rid of this and the car, and have an early night at home.' It would make a pleasant change after the last few hectic weeks to be able to laze for an hour or two.

The passenger lounge was full, and she negotiated her way through the international cross-section of humanity that frequents every airport waiting room in the world, making her way with as much speed as was possible in such congested conditions towards the door marked 'Exit' in three languages.

Avoiding a harassed mother with a strident voice, and four unruly children who appeared deaf to the penetrating nature of her utterances, Sherry side-stepped a portly clergyman, and halted in mid-stride as a disembodied voice fell from the loudspeakers fixed to the ceiling beams above their heads. It announced in impersonal, B.B.C. English that owing to winds approaching gale force, incoming flights were being diverted to other airports. Outgoing flights, it said tinnily, would be temporarily grounded, and passengers conveyed by road to an airport forty miles further south, where the services were still able to operate.

It was a run that Sherry had made many times before for the same reason, the location of the other airport being less at the mercy of the elements than this high, exposed plateau that was situated among the Border hills, and served as a handy intermediate changing house for most of the big airlines operating between the main termini of the northern and southern capitals.

The voice added the obvious rider that as soon as the weather conditions improved, normal services would be resumed, and ended with the usual apology for any inconvenience caused, etc. A murmur of dismay rippled through the passengers grouped round the lounge, and the strident voice increased in volume. Stifling a feeling of guilt that the misfortune of these people would mean profit to them, Sherry dodged round the clergyman, avoided two leap-frogging children, and gained the fresh air with a gasp of relief. The contrast in atmosphere was tremendous after the

6

stifling heat of the lounge, and she stood for a minute to fill her lungs with the clear, cold wind that whistled across the open downland in breath-stopping gusts, rudely tossing her short auburn hair into miniature ringlets about her heart-shaped face.

Humming lightly to herself, she tucked her bright scarf more closely into the collar of her short motor coat, glad of the wind-stopping properties of suede, for the gusts had in them an icy bite that spoke of their north-eastern origin, and ran down the entrance steps to the large grey saloon that waited for her at the foot. She ducked inside thankfully, tossed the case into the back, and slammed the door against the noise of the wind. Without pausing to make herself comfortable she reached forward and flicked a switch on the dashboard.

'Ben?'

She spoke into the radio receiving set fixed conveniently among the instruments confronting her.

'Yes, Miss Sherry?'

The voice of the elderly mechanic back at the garage answered her. It sounded slightly muffled, and Sherry smiled. She had disturbed Ben at his mid-afternoon snack. It would be fruit cake that had gone down in the middle. Ben's wife was not the world's most accomplished cook, but her husband cheerfully accepted the inevitable, and a slice of doughy cake each afternoon, and seemed to thrive on the results.

'The airport will be calling for coaches any minute now.' Quickly she told him what she had heard. 'Have two of ours filled up ready, will you? Oh, and you might warn Dee Lawrence's foreman to lay on a van in case there's too much luggage. There usually is,' she said resignedly.

'Right away, miss!' There was the sound of a gulp, and the sharp clack of a cup being put down hastily in a saucer, and Sherry flicked the radio off, confident that Ben would have the vehicles ready for the road when the call came. It did not do to keep the airport waiting. Humphrey Manders had built up a considerable amount of goodwill with the people in charge there by his speedy and reliable response to their calls for help, and she did not want anything to go wrong while she was left in charge of his fleet. Particularly, she did not want to have to ask Dee Lawrence to intervene in any difficulties that she might encounter while her uncle was away. She still smarted under the knowledge that Dee had been asked to keep a general eye on things while she was in control, when she knew herself to be capable of running the business on her own.

'I ought to know how,' she had told Humphrey Manders, 'after all, you taught me yourself,' she added unarguably.

It had not been an easy apprenticeship. Her uncle did not suffer fools gladly, and when she finally finished school and returned home to Arne Cottage to live, she insisted on earning her own living, and he had proceeded to teach her the business from the bottom, as if she had been a nephew instead of a niece. Starting at the switchboard-cum-transmitting set that controlled the movements of the radio-fitted cars, she graduated through every facet of keeping a fleet of cars and coaches on the road fifty-two weeks of the year. At first, her efforts won her a tolerant indulgence from the men in the garage, most of whom had watched her grow up, but this rapidly turned to respect as ability, backed by sheer hard work, made her an increasingly useful member of Humphrey Manders' team.

Typically, because she was his own flesh and blood, he had driven Sherry harder than any of his staff, almost as hard as he drove himself, and she had responded eagerly, glad to be able to pull her weight at last, and repay her uncle in some small way for the care he had lavished on her since, when she was a lively three-year-old, he had brought her to Arne Cottage, insisting on his right to bring up his orphan niece with the help of Polly Flint, his housekeeper. Even his sister had to admit that for a bachelor he had done a good job, though she was vocally opposed to Sherry driving 'those taxi things', as she disparagingly called his proud fleet of limousines.

'It isn't a job for a girl, Charlotte.'

Aunt Hatty never, ever, called her Sherry, that happy diminutive occasioned by her lovely amber hair and eyes that had stuck since she had first toddled into Humphrey Manders' home and heart, and had remained firmly fixed in both ever since.

'It's perfectly safe,' protested Sherry. 'It isn't as if our cars stand on a taxi rank and pick up any stray who wants a ride. All our trips are phoned bookings. And I'm quite capable of looking after myself,' she declared confidently, unaware that her slender form and tiny, heart-shaped face that made her look several years younger than she really was did nothing to reassure her anxious relative.

Upon receiving the news of her brother's illness, Hatty Manders had arrived post-haste at Arne Cottage, intent on carrying him back home to Devon with her, to nurse him back to fitness after his mild heart attack. A warning, the doctors had called it, adding another that he dared not ignore, and recommending a period of complete rest.

The owner of Manders Motors viewed the prospect of a couple of months of his sister's tender care with base ingratitude, and openly fretted about the prospect of such a prolonged absence from his garage.

'Businesses don't run themselves. And it's not a job for a girl,' he shot at Sherry as she opened her mouth to protest, for the hundredth time, that she could look after things for him until he came back. 'It's a rough enough job for a man,' he added ruefully, still smarting after a recent encounter with his sorely tried physician.

So it was with growing surprise that Sherry watched his meek capitulation, as her aunt packed his things a mere two days later. His continued mild acceptance worried her at first, then as his health obviously continued to improve it sowed a seed of suspicion in her mind that flourished mightily as the hours passed without the expected explosion, and burst into luxurious bloom when he announced calmly, the evening before his departure.

'I've taught you all I can. Now's your chance to put what you've learned into practice.'

'You won't be on your own really, Charlotte,' her aunt fluttered ill-timed comfort, 'you can always ring us in Devon . . .'

'She won't be on her own anyway,' retorted Humphrey Manders blandly, 'Dee Lawrence has promised to keep an eye on her.'

Sherry set her engine running, and stifled the flash of annoyance that coursed through her every time she thought of being supervised by Dee. He was barely five years older than she was, twenty-nine at the most, and she did not need him to act as a nursemaid while her uncle was away, she told herself vexedly, easing the big car out of the airport gates and accelerating on to the smooth tarmac of the main road for the long run back to Beacon Downs. She did not even know Dee particularly well except as a business neighbour. His tall, spare figure was familiar enough on his occasional visits to Manders Motors, when for some reason he wanted to hire one of the cars; for Beacon Hire, which he owned, was a goods carrying service only, running vans and lorries, and the two firms hired from one another when necessary rather than keep rarely-used vehicles lying idle on their own premises. When Dee wanted something he always dealt directly with her uncle, never with Sherry herself, and although he always spoke courteously enough to her whenever he met her in the yard or the office, he never seemed to have either the time or the inclination to stop for more than his customary smiling hello as he passed. Her own increasing driving activities kept her away from their own garage quite a lot, and it had been some time since she had set eyes on him, which did nothing to make the situation between them any more acceptable to her now.

By their very nature, the two businesses were complementary, and without the need for competition between them they co-existed happily enough. They would continue to do so, thought Sherry mutinously, just so long as Dee Lawrence kept to Beacon Hire, and left her to look after Manders Motors.

A screeching gust of wind hit the car broadside on, and despite its size it shivered like a live thing under her hands, emptying Sherry's head of any thought except that of keeping safely on the road as it climbed steadily like a dark shoelace across the face of the open hillside, rising towards the summit before it dropped steeply on the other side, and then rose again for the short, sharp climb up to the old walled town of Beacon Downs. Sherry settled back in her seat, her hands firm on the wheel, her senses alert to the very real danger of unexpected body blows dealt by the capricious wind on the solid sides of the big car, that had caused many an incautious driver to regret allowing his thoughts to wander on such an exposed piece of road.

The long grey bonnet rose over the top of the hill, then dipped, allowing her the view on the other side. The town of Beacon Downs lay in front of her, toy-sized, perched on the top of its hill like a miniature fortress such as would find its way into many a small boy's Christmas parcel in a few weeks' time, thought Sherry with a smile. The battlemented walls stood out boldly, looking deceptively close in the clear winter air, and even at this distance the grey surface of Battle Pools, the three great sheets of water fed by the River Arne as it flowed through the valley floor, making a paradise for the wild fowl that flighted in each night from the high downland to rest in safety among its flanking reeds, looked ruffled by the bitter, hurtling wind.

Two small pencil marks of darkness crawled slowly along the road beside the pools, followed by a bright orange dot, and Sherry knew that Ben must have received the expected call from the airport, and turned out two coaches. The orange dot would be one of Dee's big vans, so Ben had warned his foreman as she had asked him to. Sherry's resentment at what she felt to be unwarranted interference on Dee's part did not extend to jeopardizing their business relationship. That was an impersonal thing, and valuable to them both.

She toed the accelerator, increasing speed as the shoulder of the hill sheltered her from the wind on the downward grade, and swiftly the approaching vehicles took on shape and size. Three sets of headlights flashed recognition, and three hands were each raised in turn to her own response as the vehicles passed on the other side. Sherry smiled, warmed as she always was by the brief human encounter on the road. Driving was often a very lonely occupation.

The low parapet of the river bridge fled towards her and she checked her speed, eyeing the approaching road junction on the other side. It was bare of traffic, and her eyes widened as she caught sight of what from the distance had appeared to be ruffled water on the surface of the pools. Close under her wheels now, the ruffles turned into high, angry waves that built and broke unceasingly under the riotous air, and it was not hard to visualize on this stormy winter's day how the area had gained its name. A wooden road sign lay tossed on its side at the junction.

'Probably fallen off one of the Council lorries,' surmised Sherry, 'it's not surprising in this wind.'

She took the fork that led to the West Gate, arching high above her at the top of the steeply rising road. The graceful opening looked as welcome to her now as it must have done to the foot travellers centuries ago. There would be shelter within the walls of the town from the tearing wind that scoured the helpless grass on the downland outside. A quick trip to the Royal Hotel to get rid of the case, straight to the garage to swap cars, and then she would be at home in front of the fire, and there would be no more battling with traffic, business, or the elements until the morning. The lack of traffic on the approach to the West Gate struck her as odd, it was usually a busy road, and she slowed as a burly figure in dungarees stood out in the centre of the carriageway and held up his hand.

'Can't you read, miss?'

'Read what?'

A spark of temper rose inside her at the man's tone, and her lips tightened.

'There's a sign at the junction sez "Diversion",' the owner of the hand informed her, 'we've got an 'ole 'ere.'

From the look of his hand and overalls, most of the contents seemed to have transferred themselves to him, thought Sherry, but she forced a conciliatory note into her voice when she replied:

'I saw a sign blown face down on the side of the road,' she returned quietly. 'I thought it had fallen off a lorry.'

'If you'd 'ave looked, you'd 'ave seen it said "Diversion",' the dungareed one told her with satisfaction.

Sherry did not see how that would have helped. The sign had been tossed on to the verge, and if she had picked it up and read it she would have had no way of knowing where it had originally pointed. She was about to explain this when the burly roadman stepped back.

'Seein' as you're 'ere, you might as well go on,' he told her grudgingly, 'but go slow, we've got an 'ole 'ere.'

He seemed to think a lot of his hole.

'I'll treat it with the greatest respect,' Sherry assured him gravely, and was rewarded by his look of open-mouthed puzzlement as she changed down and crawled towards it. He had understated his case, she decided two seconds later. It was not a hole, it was a trench, and it stretched from one side of the West Gate to the other. It was also fairly deep. She hesitated, glancing back to see if there was any traffic following

14

her, and caught sight of the open grin on the face of the workman. That decided her. Instantly she slipped into bottom gear, and eased the car forward. The minute the front wheels hit the trench she regretted her impulse, but it was too late now. Exerting pressure from the high-powered engine, she pushed the nose out and gentled the rear end downwards. It bottomed heavily, and she winced.

'I hope to goodness I haven't done any damage,' she thought worriedly. It was useless to wish she had backed off now, and with a piece of expert driving she extricated the car and increased speed, thankful when a sharp turn hid the still grinning roadman from sight.

It took her another ten minutes to worm her way through the snarled-up traffic in the town centre, negotiating narrow, cobbled streets that had been designed for carrying mounted men in the days of the first Elizabeth, before she reached the Royal Hotel and thankfully handed the suitcase over to the porter.

'A waste of money, if you asks me,' he commented, echoing Sherry's own sentiments. She laughed.

'Not entirely, Alf, it helps to keep us on the road,' she reminded him, thankful as always that the hotel forecourt, cobbled like the streets outside, was built on spacious lines. A coach and horses needed a generous turning circle, and the inherited space was a definite advantage in spinning the big car round to get out. There was never any need to shunt at the Royal, she thought gratefully. She lifted a hand in response to the porter's friendly wave, and returned to face the traffic, slipping into the flow with an easy familiarity that made light of the complicated one-way system that was the Town Council's only means of reconciling ancient and modern.

She turned the nose of the car into the steepening rise of Hay Market Street, wondering, as she always did, how the huge drays with their sweet-smelling loads ever managed to struggle up the incline to the open square at the top, where generations ago the produce of the district was bought and sold, and where now fountains played, and made the square a pleasant place to rest while shopping on a summer's day. The traffic lights showed green as she approached the crossroads, and she wondered if they would hold until she got to them. Her luck was out, the amber warning flashed, and as she approached the white line the top light shone red. Her foot reached automatically for the brake pedal, at the same time as the fingers of her left hand closed round the gear lever. It took precisely two seconds for her mind to register the fact that the brake was not working. Her foot slammed hard against the floorboards, and was met with a flaccid lack of pressure from the pedal that told its own tale. The trench at the West Gate had taken its toll.

Out of the corner of her eye she saw a large orange shape accelerating up the street on her left, gaining speed to catch the lights while they were still green. Unable to stop the big car, Sherry acted instinctively, her years behind the wheel giving her an automatic response that had no need of conscious thought. Simultaneously she thrust the gear lever down and her foot on the accelerator. The great grey vehicle leapt forward like a startled horse pricked by a spur. The orange van was almost on top of her, and Sherry ducked, shrinking from the impact that seemed inevitable. An anguished screeching of brakes tore the air, a man's voice shouted, and miraculously she was across the lights, and the orange van was hurtling by behind her with only the thickness of a coat of paint to spare.

Momentum kept her car moving for a yard or two, and she let it go to clear the traffic lights, drawing into the kerb on the other side and allowing the natural pull of the incline to slow her to a halt. She pulled the handbrake tight, mercifully that was working, then switched off the engine and put the car into gear as an extra precaution. With a quick look to check that the flow of traffic could get round her she reached up to unhook her seat belt, conscious that her fingers trembled. With a wary eye on some approaching cars she slid out of the door, and looked round for the orange van. It, too, had drawn up to the kerb on the other side of the intersection, and Sherry gave a groan of dismay as she saw a tall, lean figure open the door and drop to the ground. Of all people to have a near miss with, she had to choose Dee Lawrence! He slammed his door shut and crossed the junction towards her with swift, athletic strides that somehow conveyed his opinion of her driving even before his angry blue eyes bored into her own from at least a foot above her head.

'They're the blue of periwinkles,' thought Sherry inconsequentially. She had never noticed what colour his eyes were before.

'What the blazes do you mean, trying to jump the lights like that? Do you want to get yourself killed?'

'I couldn't ...'

'You deliberately accelerated as they turned to red,' he accused her furiously. 'If the cobbles had been wet, my brakes would never have held. No wonder your uncle was worried about leaving you to look after things while he was away,' he said scornfully. 'If this is the way you drive you ought not to hold a licence!'

Sherry went white. Her normally pale skin lost all the colour it had, and her eyes blazed.

'I'd like to know what else I could have done with a failed brake!' she blazed. 'If I'd . . .'

'A failed – what?'

'Don't interrupt.' She stamped her foot, beside herself with temper, oblivious of a knot of interested pedestrians and a rapidly looming policeman. 'When my footbrake wouldn't work I had to accelerate to get past you, otherwise you would have gone straight into the nearside of my car. Perhaps you would have preferred that,' she bit scathingly, 'then you would have had every excuse to take control of Manders Motors while my uncle is away.' All the resentment she felt at his being asked to keep an eye on the business during her uncle's absence boiled up inside her, and she spoke wildly, barbing her words, and uncaring where they fell.

Dee ran a brown hand through his hair, fluffing the fair curls into distracted tufts.

'I didn't know . . .' he started, completely taken aback by the fury of her attack.

'You didn't stop to find out,' she returned swiftly.

'Let me give you a tow.' His voice was quiet now, his face withdrawn. Her shot about his taking control of Manders Motors had told.

'I'll get a lift in from our own garage.' Curtly she refused him, turning her back and sliding into her driving seat, her hand reaching out for the radio switch.

'Ben?'

'Here, Miss Sherry.'

'Send out the crash wagon, will you? I'm stuck by the traffic lights in Haymarket Street,' she told him. 'My brakes have failed.'

'Are you all right, miss?' Ben's voice sounded anxious.

'Yes, no harm done,' Sherry replied crisply, hoping that Dee did not notice how her fingers still trembled. 'I hit a hole in the road under the West Gate, and it looks as if the pipe carrying the brake fluid might have fractured. There's no pressure on the pedal.' She emphasized the trouble maliciously, conscious that Dee still stood by the car door, and she saw him stiffen.

'I can't send out the wagon for a bit, Miss Sherry,' Ben's voice was concerned. 'It's bringing in one of Mr. Lawrence's vans. There's a lot of glass been broken at the bottom end of the town, and his driver had two tyres go, so I guessed you'd want me to give him a hand.'

Ben had only done what she would have instructed him to if she had been back at the garage, and Sherry knew it. But why, oh, why did it have to happen now?

'You'll have to get your car moved, miss.' A blue-uniformed figure blocked out the light of her driving window, and Sherry turned. A policeman, even taller than Dee, and a lot burlier, bent to peer in at her, and she stuck her head out of the window. 'When the traffic builds up about five o'clock it'll cause an obstruction here.'

'How they love official language,' thought Sherry crossly, her normal sense of fairness vanished in the face of her dilemma. 'Our own crash wagon will be here in about half an hour . . .' she began, when Dee interrupted.

'I'll give her a tow back. My van is big enough to take the pull, and our premises are adjacent.' He spoke

19

to the policeman rather than to Sherry.

'I'd be glad if you would, sir,' that officer returned with relief. 'It gets bad here, about commuter time.'

Sherry could have told him that, she had driven through the snarled-up tangle herself often enough to avoid it if she possibly could, and knew just what hold-ups a lame vehicle could cause in the double stream along the narrow streets, but just now she felt she would rather have risked that than accept a tow from Dee. He did not wait to hear if she had any objection. With a nod to the policeman he turned away, and in minutes the large orange van was pulled up a short distance in front of her, and he was uncoiling a tow rope from the back.

'Trust him to be prepared,' fumed Sherry unjustly, ignoring the fact that their own cars always went out supplied with tow ropes and other emergency measures in the boot. Stubbornly she sat tight, refusing to help, though his experienced hands needed none, and in seconds a length of tough nylon rope was firmly fixed between her own car and the van. Dee came to her door, and his face was tight.

'I'm ready for off. When I hoot, put her into neutral.' His eyes took in the position of the gear lever. 'There's no need for you to wait for your own crash wagon,' he finished.

'You can send in the bill,' Sherry snapped ungraciously, and he flushed.

'For two pins I will. If you've got no more sense than to take a fine vehicle like this through that trench under the West Gate, you deserve to have to pay for the damage.' His voice grated his opinion of anyone who ill-used machinery, and he snapped her door shut, turning on his heel to gain his own driving seat with a swift pull up into the high vehicle. Sherry saw the van vibrate as he switched on the ignition, heard his horn signal once, and acknowledged the policeman's wave as he turned them both into the carriageway with one hand, while holding up the traffic stream with his other.

Sherry slipped her gears and the handbrake, and turned in Dee's wake as she felt the pull of the rope urge the car forward, her natural driving instinct submerging her indignation, though she still simmered at the way in which he had turned her own remarks against her. Telling Ben what had caused the trouble had been a mistake, but it was one she could not rectify now, and at least Dee Lawrence knew where he stood as regards her own position, she thought unrepentantly.

She kept her eyes alert to the danger of someone trying to cross the roped space between the two vehicles, conscious of pedestrians walking head down against the wind, and consequently even more unobservant than usual. It hit them with renewed force once they were out of the confines of the shopping centre. Sherry saw the van in front of her stagger under the buffeting of one particularly bad gust, its high sides offering greater resistance than the low car she was driving, although even that swayed.

'We're in for a wild night,' she thought, anxious now to get home for she knew that Polly hated storms. Although the elderly housekeeper presented a stern, unbending front to the world, Sherry suspected that she harboured a strong streak of superstition, and she was never really easy during the frequent gales that hit the high-sited little town at this time of the year.

Ben saw them coming and he was at the double iron

gates waiting for them, swinging them wide in the fading light, and fussing round the car as she brought it to a standstill like a hen about a lame chick. Sherry knew that he would not rest until he had got it road-worthy again. With Paul, the young apprentice, he would work on until he was satisfied it could be safely turned out again in the morning. Sherry glanced into the corner of the garage, and saw that the crash wagon was back in its usual place. That meant Dee's van would be under service too, the same as her car. She could see the dark outlines of a van on the hoist in his workshop across the road, the open doors letting out a yellow pool of light into the darkening afternoon. Ben caught her glance.

'That's the one we brought in this afternoon.' He nodded towards the premises opposite theirs. 'I'll have yours ready for you by to . . .'

The rest of his sentence was lost in a roaring gust of wind that whipped up the street as if it was a funnel, and hit the two garage buildings on either side with a solid force that seemed to rattle their very foundations. It caught Sherry off balance and spun her off her feet as if she was a feather. She grabbed at the door handle of the car, missed, and felt a pair of hard arms go round her as their owner backed against the solid surface of the vehicle behind them.

'Thanks, Ben,' Sherry gasped gratefully, looking up at the face above her.

'It isn't Ben, it's me.'

A pair of periwinkle blue eyes regarded her amus-edly, and Dee put his lips close to her ear to make her hear against the force of the gale. He said something else, but although Sherry saw his lips move his voice disappeared in an awful cracking, grinding sound that came from his own building across the road. She wrenched herself round in his arms, felt them tighten their hold, drawing her close against him as together they watched the asbestos roof of the Beacon Hire Company lift from its moorings, sail like a kite over the open area of the yard, and collapse as the wind suddenly withdrew its support, engulfing the entire length of the stout iron fencing surrounding the premises.

CHAPTER TWO

As if in a dream, Sherry watched the railings buckle under the downward thrust of the heavy weight resting on top of them. They seemed to bend slowly, like something in a slow-motion film, and settled at a crazy angle as one end of the structure came to rest on the ground and took part of its own weight. Tearing noises split the air as pieces broke away, to be grasped in their turn by the destructive fingers of the gale and whirled in every direction.

'Duck!'

Hard hands thrust her downwards, and her knees buckled like the railings under their desperate force. The hard concrete of the yard bit cold through the legs of her trouser suit, and Dee was pressing her relentlessly down, leaning over her so that she could not move had she wished. The cosy softness of a cashmere sweater brushed against her cheek, and she turned her head to ease an uncomfortable crick in her neck. She could feel his heart beating under the fine wool, and wished the button that adorned it had not been so hard, it hurt her ear where she pressed against him.

A loud crash of glass made her forget her ear, and she heard Dee swear softly, the vibration of his voice rumbling through his chest. Trembling, and hardly able to breathe with the pressure of his hold upon her, an aeon passed before she felt him stir. The pressure eased, and she sat up rubbing her ear. The same hands that had held her down now lifted her gently, setting her on her feet, and his voice, all the sharpness gone from it, spoke above her head.

'Phew! That was close!'

Bemused, she realized that she could hear him, that he was not shouting. The gust had died, and left behind it an uncanny silence. A gentle creaking came from the wreckage of the roof where the wind rocked it against the railings, and Sherry turned her head. Ben emerged from behind the car where he had ducked out of the way, his chubby, wide-eyed stare reminiscent of one of the dwarfs in *Snow White*. Sherry felt a hysterical giggle start inside her, and stamped on it ruthlessly. Hysterics would help no one now. She felt a cold shiver run through her as her eyes traced the cause of the smashed glass. A huge piece of asbestos, bristling with jagged steel struts, had hurled through the big windows of the workshop and wedged itself inside the frame with force enough to splinter the heavy wood. If that had hit them . . . She shuddered.

Dee felt her tremble, and put an arm about her.

'It didn't happen,' he pointed out obviously. He tried to speak lightly, but the shock sounded in his voice, and a bleak look tightened his thin face as he surveyed the wreckage of his premises. It seemed dark, and Sherry realized that the pool of light from the workshop across the road had vanished. She could hear men's voices, and Dee bent his head.

'Stay with Ben, Sherry. I'm going over to see if everyone is all right.'

She noticed he said 'everyone', his first thought being for his men.

'I'm coming with you.'

'Me, too,' said Ben, appearing beside them, a stout and comforting silhouette.

Dee did not argue. With long strides he crossed the

yard and made for the gate into the road.

'Mind the spars here, they're blocking half the pavement.'

- He climbed over a tangle of shattered roofing and turned, with both hands held out to help her across. Sherry grasped them thankfully, conscious of the steel strength of his slim fingers as they curled about her own. She leapt nimbly across the mess, her lighter weight carrying her over the wreckage with greater ease than the two men. Ben made heavier weather of it, and Dee left her to wait for the elderly mechanic, hastening into the workshop where Sherry could hear his voice calling out strongly.

'We're all right, guv'nor. We're in here!'

There were puzzled sounds from Dee, a scraping, and a clink of metal as if he had bumped into tools or something lying on the floor, then a burst of laughter. Did that, too, hold a faint note of hysteria? Sherry's ears, sharpened by the darkness, detected a world of relief in the sound. She made cautiously towards it, unconsciously hanging on to Ben by his overall belt, as she had done when she was small.

'Mind where you step.' Dee's voice was quite calm now. 'There's an inspection pit in the floor here.'

A faint glow of light appeared almost underneath her feet, and Sherry checked her progress hastily. It was the first time she had ever been on the premises of Beacon Hire. The thin pencil beam of torchlight widened, and she looked down on a row of upturned faces, crowded into the deep workshop inspection pit. Ben gave a rumble of laughter behind her.

'Not a bad place to shelter, eh?' He turned to Dee. 'Have you got a ladder, guv'nor? If we can get them out of there we can start clearing up for you.' He took it

26

for granted that Sherry would agree to his helping.

Wordlessly, Dee leaned down and borrowed the torch, swinging the light into a corner where several ladders hung on hooks along the wall. He lifted one down and let it carefully into the pit, and within minutes several men were grouped about him.

'See if you can rig up some sort of light, will you?' Dee spoke to one whom Sherry recognized as his foreman. 'I'll go and check if the phones are still working.'

Sherry surveyed the pollarded second storey, standing starkly against the sky like the photograph of a bombed building. She knew that Dee had his office there, and a flat at one end which, being a bachelor, he found adequate for his needs, being serviced by the daily who coped in the garage, and useful in that it kept him literally on top of his work. It was approached by a spartan iron staircase running down the outside of the building, similar to a fire escape, and Sherry spoke impulsively.

'Don't go up the stairs. They may not be safe.'

'I'll be careful.' He gave her an inscrutable look, paused as if he was going to say something else, then turned away without speaking and made for the bottom of the steps. It took him a long time to get there, he had to pick his way through the debris littering the yard, and Sherry held her breath as his feet scraped on the iron steps. Somehow, she did not know why, she expected him to mount the stairs two at a time as she had seen him do many times before, and she let her breath out in a sigh of relief as he trod cautiously, a step at a time, keeping to the side of the wall, and testing each step before risking his full weight upon it. He reached the top, and ducked through the hole where the door had been, and disappeared inside. He seemed to be gone for a long time. Sherry could see him now and then as his figure became outlined in the gaunt, empty window spaces, and then he reappeared, running lightly down the steps.

'The phones are gone,' he announced. 'Do you mind if I use yours? I shall have to let the police know, because of the blockage in the road.'

'I'll ring them for you,' Sherry offered. 'You go ahead and attend to things here. I'll come back when I've got through.'

He nodded, and Sherry turned and made her way back towards the gate. It was easier going this time, Dee's men had already made an inroad into the tangle that blocked the passage, and she hurried through it. Letting herself into her office, she reached for the instrument on her desk, relieved to hear the dialling tone as soon as she lifted the receiver. She dialled quickly, using the emergency number, and reported the trouble to the friendly voice that answered her from the other end.

'We'll send someone over, miss.' How comforting the police always sounded, she thought. 'How is Mr. Lawrence managing about clearing up the damage?'

'He's got some of his men with him, and one of mine. There is no one hurt,' replied Sherry thankfully, 'and they're starting in on the mess now.'

She dropped the receiver back on its hook, and turned to find Ben in the doorway.

'I'm going to rig up some lights on our railings, Miss Sherry. We can run them off the generator here. With a bit of light on the scene the clearing up will be done a lot quicker. At least we can get the mess off the road for tonight, and leave the damage inside until it's light in the morning.'

'I'm going back to give Mr. Lawrence a hand.'

She left Ben to it and hurried back across the road. Dee poked his head out of what was left of an upstairs window, and Sherry called to him.

'I'm coming up.'

'Bring some plastic sheeting with you,' he shouted back. 'There's a stack of it in a corner by the ladders.'

Sherry lifted her hand, not bothering to raise her own voice against the wind, and hurried back into the garage where he directed. Carefully skirting the inspection pit, illumined now by the torch which had been left on a nearby bench for the purpose, she sought the corner where Dee had taken the ladder from, and found the pile of plastic sheeting, neatly bundled and tied, in a small wired enclosure. The squares of heavy duty plastic had been made up ready in sheets, with a bundle of twine for tying down in a net at the side. Someone believed in being prepared, thought Sherry approvingly, and picked up the net and as many as she could hold of the plastic sheets. Dee met her struggling up the iron stairway with her arms full, and relieved her of the sheeting.

When they got to the door at the top he stepped aside and waved her in, his natural courtesy showing even in these circumstances. Light flooded suddenly through the glassless holes in the walls, and a ragged cheer from down below announced Ben's success in rigging up some form of lighting on their own railings. It would speed up the work in the road, but up here, in what had been Dee's office, it only served to highlight the havoc surrounding them. Broken glass was everywhere, crunching into the floor strewn with scattered papers and up-ended furniture. Sherry turned towards Dee, her eyes wide with dismay.

'Things are a bit upside down at the moment, I'm afraid.' He sounded like a housewife excusing a littered living room to an unexpected guest, and catching the wry quirk of his lips in the uncertain light Sherry laughed shakily.

'I'll take you as I find you,' she said graciously, astounded at her companion's resilience in the face of what could be ruinous repair expenses.

'Let's get the rooms in the flat covered first.' Dee opened a door in one corner of the office and walked through first, thrusting aside debris to make a passageway for her. 'Mind your head!' He ducked under a hanging spar of metal, and Sherry found herself in a minute hall. The office had had nothing but the bare metal spars and the asbestos sheets of the roof above the working area, but this was covered by a ceiling. She followed him into what appeared to be his living room, and found that, too, was fitted with the same facility. Richly embossed paper threw minute shadows on the stark white of it, from the light of Ben's lamps, and Sherry felt as if she had stepped into a different world. There was not so much damage here, the ceiling had prevented the full force of the gale from entering the room, though in several places large areas of it hung down from gaping holes, swinging menacingly above their heads.

Sherry had always imagined that a man's bachelor flat would be a spartan affair, of litter, and unwashed crocks in the sink, but here was evidence of a man's love of good things, and comfortable living. A carpet, richly coloured and deeply soft, received her feet in luxurious comfort, and the tweed-covered armchairs, several in the spacious area of the room, invited a quiet evening with a book, of which there was a plentiful supply lining the walls. In the light from the lamps outside Sherry caught one or two of the titles on the nearest shelf, betraying the owner's interest that several skilful pen-and-ink sketches of wild birds, now hung crazily askew on the walls, confirmed. Dee caught her glance.

'I can do some more if those are spoiled,' he said indifferently, shaking out one of the plastic sheets, and handing the other end to Sherry. 'Drape it over the chairs, will you, and if we tie the ends down to the legs it should prevent any damage if it rains. We'll just have to cover the carpet up with one or two and hope for the best.'

Silently Sherry did as she was bid, her thoughts on the pictures. So Dee sketched. She had never known him well enough to be aware of his hobbies. Until now their contact had been purely business, and she felt confused, and rather out of her depth to be confronted suddenly with the man behind the brisk, businesslike exterior, and the impersonal hello thrown in passing, that was all she had known of him until tonight. She hesitated outside his bedroom door, but he handed her an end of another plastic sheet and carried on in himself, perforce dragging her behind him. This room was the worst hit, being on the end of the building, and its condition was a disaster. Most of the ceiling was in bits on the floor, the smoke blue and grey of the carpet barely visible under a thick coating of dust and debris, mixed with vicious spears of glass from a shattered dressing-table mirror in the corner.

'There's not much we can do here, I'm afraid, except cover it over until tomorrow and leave it as it is.'

He suited action to his words, shaking out the plastic over the top of the nearest furniture, dodging underneath the dark blue velvet curtains that ironically still hung with their former elegance against the ivory-coloured walls. Sherry unfolded another length of plastic and drew it over the bed.

'Leave that.' Dee raised his head from his own task and saw what she was doing.

'What if it rains?'

'Let's hope it won't,' he said fervently, 'I've got to sleep somewhere.'

'You can't stay the night here!' Sherry stared at him aghast. The bitter north-east wind whistled through the roofless room, sparing no corner from its icy, searching fingers. Her own felt numb with its passing.

'This is the only room with no ceiling left to collapse,' Dee shrugged. 'And the garage workshop doesn't boast a bed.'

'You'll freeze to death!'

Sherry knew what her uncle would have done in the circumstances, and however much it went against the grain, she could do no less.

'Come home with me. There's a spare room at Arne Cottage, and I'll give Polly a ring.' There was more than one spare room at home. The house that had been designated 'cottage' boasted five good-sized bedrooms, and with Humphrey Manders in Devon, only hers and Polly's were in use.

Dee straightened from his task of tying down a sheet, his face level with her own. His eyes were quizzical, black in the uncertain light.

'If you really mean that?'

'Of course I mean it!' Sherry shook her sheet briskly

across the top of the bed and refused to meet his look. 'Uncle Humph would be furious if he thought you'd stayed here instead of being comfortable with us.' It was the farthest she could make herself go, but it evidently convinced Dee, because he nodded, satisfied.

'In that case, thanks, I will.'

'Will you want any – things?' Sherry felt awkward. She did not want to offer him a pair of her uncle's pyjamas. Apart from being about six sizes too wide, it stuck in her throat to offer him Humphrey Manders' clothes. He had been asked to keep an eye on the business, not to step into its owner's shoes – or in this case his pyjamas. Despite their situation Sherry's lips twitched. Quickly she bent to tie the sheet to the bed, hiding her ill-timed amusement. She heard drawers opening behind her, and the sound of hands hastily sorting through the contents. They slammed shut, and Dee's voice came from across the room:

'At least I shan't have to get my suitcase from the top of the wardrobe. The wind has done that much for me.'

She turned, her task completed, all trace of laughter gone from her face. Looking at him across the wreckage it did not seem a laughing matter. He picked up a small suitcase from the floor, shook it free from plaster chippings, and snapped it open, stuffing something that looked like sky-blue silk inside. Dumping it on top of the bed, he disappeared through a doorway at the end of the room, and again there was the sound of a drawer opening and shutting. A dark-coloured toilet bag, bulging at the sides, followed the first bundle into the case, and with a cautious tug Dee reached out and forced open the wardrobe door, not an easy task as it hung drunkenly across the dressing-table, only saved from falling by the narrowness of the space between the two pieces of furniture. As soon as there was a gap sufficiently wide to take his hand he reached inside, felt around for a minute, then juggled with something that sounded like a metal coat-hanger. His hand came out grasping a dark, soft-looking dressing-gown. He shook it out, folded it over his arm, and turned towards her.

'Shall we go?'

Unexpectedly, Sherry blushed. A warm tide of colour rose from her throat, suffusing the delicate pallor of her cheeks richly pink. Unable to stop herself, she put a hand to her cheek, wishing for the first time that Ben had not been so successful in rigging up his battery of lights. From down below the hum of the generator came through strongly, offering an ample supply of power. There was no lack of light now. Sherry turned away quickly, but not in time to prevent Dee from seeing her face. She felt his fingers close round her arm, and despite herself she stiffened.

'Mind the rubble here, it's a bit shaky,' was all he said, and he helped her across the doorway into the other room with solicitous care, but his eyes as they met hers, briefly, unwillingly on Sherry's part, held an amusement that brought a quick spark of temper to her own. She hurried over the pile of ceiling spars, tripped and would have fallen had his arm not reached out and grasped her firmly, much as he had done in the yard earlier on.

'Hold hard!' he admonished her, 'the ceiling isn't likely to collapse for a bit.'

He must think she was afraid of the roof falling in, she thought with relief, wondering what it was she *had* been afraid of. What had caused the sudden feeling of panic to well up inside her, and die just as suddenly as it had come, so that she wondered now if it had been there at all? He kept his hand lightly on her shoulder, guiding her through the big living room, but his touch no longer confused her, and her colour returned to normal.

'What a shame! Your sketches . . .'

She pointed to a set of three, hung in a dropping line along the wall, their plain wooden frames tilted all ways by the gale.

'Take one with you.'

Dee reached out and plucked the nearest one from its hook. It was a picture of a small owl. He looked at it thoughtfully for a moment, then with a quick, decided shake of his head he returned it to its place.

'No, take this one instead.'

He removed the next one to it from the wall.

'This one suits you better.'

He thrust the small frame into Sherry's hands and she looked down, marvelling at the skill of the penmanship that quickened into life the minute jenny wren looking back at her from beneath the glass, its eyes brightly alert, and perky tail upright as a guardsman behind its back. She smiled back at the pictured miniature, pleased with her unexpected present, and wondered why the small wren should suit her better than the soft, fluffy picture of the owl. They both looked equally attractive to her.

Dee followed her out through the hall, across the shattered office, and on to the iron staircase outside. Sherry shivered, and drew her coat round her. It had been cold enough inside the roofless building, but out on the iron step the piercing wind took her breath away. She gripped her hands tightly together, clutching the picture against the softness of her coat.

'Never mind the jenny wren,' said Dee from behind her, mistaking her sudden movement. 'If the worst comes to the worst he can fly down,' he said dryly. 'You hold on to the hand rail or you might need wings yourself if another gust comes our way.'

His voice brought Sherry back to earth, and the precarious nature of their position, exposed on the outside of the building. Hastily she gripped the hand rail, conscious of the bitter bite of the iron against her shrinking flesh. The intermittent flash of a police light showed from a car drawn up on the other side of the road, against the gates of Manders Motors, and she could see another further along, guarding against the danger of passing traffic piling into the collapsed roofing. Ben's floodlighting illumined the area itself with a clarity which made Sherry feel proud of the elderly mechanic, whose versatility was well known in their own garage, and she could see him now at the wheel of their crash wagon, helping to winch an unwieldy piece of asbestos and steel back through the gates into the premises of Beacon Hire, in order to clear the road. Dee's own crash wagon was engaged on similar business a few yards away, and from outside the crumpled railings came the sound of energetic sawing. Sherry hesitated on the edge of the busy scene, and turned to Dee.

'Isn't there something I can do to help?'

'You've done enough,' he told her, but his voice was friendly, without the crisp, impersonal note he normally used. 'Cut across into your own office,' he bade her, 'and get out of this wind. You must be frozen.'

'I've got to ring Polly.'

'Then go and do that. I'll come for you when the men have cleared the road. It shouldn't take long, and

36

as soon as that's done we can leave the rest until day-light tomorrow.'

Sherry nodded and made her way across the road, letting herself into her own office with a sigh of relief. It was warm, almost stifling after the bitter night outside, and for two or three minutes she pressed against the hot water pipes, striving to get some feeling back into her numbed fingers. They would still hardly work the dial of the telephone when she rang Polly. Quickly she calmed the housekeeper's fears, and told her of the invitation to Dee.

'Of course you must bring him home.' Polly's voice was forthright, certain of what to do as always. 'Mr. Manders would expect you to.'

Sherry knew that, it was why she had invited him, and she tried to stifle a prick of conscience at her own reluctance to bring him into her home as well as on to their business premises. She put down the receiver and picked up the kettle. If she could not help the men labouring in the icy wind outside, she could at least make them a hot drink. A quick exploration of the kitchen used by their daily to make tea for the staff revealed a goodly supply of cups and mugs, and Sherry soon had a large brown teapot brewing on the side table. While she waited for the kettle to boil for the second time her eyes caught the picture of the wren, propped upright on her desk beside the telephone. Its chirpy look seemed to hold approval, and she began to hum as she filled the other teapot. That should be sufficient. There had been about seven of Dee's men. With Ben, four policemen, herself and Dee, fourteen cups should be enough. Rummaging in the cupboard again, she unearthed a sizeable tray, and gasped at the weight of it under the second pot of tea and fourteen cups. Hurriedly she removed both the teapots and filled the cups where they stood. Better to carry a tray of filled cups and risk some spilling than sink under the weight of that lot, she decided, mentally giving their daily help a medal until she remembered that one of the garage hands always seemed to appear conveniently about break time and carry the tray for her.

'Tea up!'

She had to raise her voice against the bluster of the wind, but it must have reached its target, for the sounds of sawing stopped as if they had been switched off, and the engines of the two crash wagons died, and their drivers appeared at Sherry's side as if by magic. Eager hands reached for her offering, and soon she was back in the office coping with refills. Dumping the depleted pots on to the table, she turned round for the tray and found Dee standing behind her.

'Sorry!' he apologized. 'Did I make you jump?'

'It's the noise of the wind, I expect. I didn't hear you come in.'

'I'll carry this for you.' He reached down and picked up the tray. 'It was a brilliant idea, bringing out a hot drink,' he approved. 'It's given the men a new lease of life, and the bobby in the Panda car has offered of his own free will to keep an eye on the place overnight for me.'

'It's on our beat anyhow, so it's no trouble,' the young officer said later as he helped stack the washed cups. Sounds of activity from outside had ceased. The road was cleared, the debris hauled back into the confines of Beacon Hire, and the men gone home. Ben had followed them after dismantling his precious lights and carefully storing them back into the stock room.

'We're off home as well, now,' remarked Sherry, giving the office door a precautionary push, and slipping the key into her pocket when she was satisfied that it held. Dee had already slung his suitcase in the van which was still parked in the yard where he drew up when he towed her car in.

'You can go home and rest easy,' said the policeman reassuringly. 'We'll keep an eye on things here for you during the night. Arne Cottage, you said?'

'Yes,' nodded Sherry, adding the phone number just in case. The Panda driver made a note of it.

'We'll contact you if it's necessary, Mr. Lawrence,' he said, 'but the wind seems to be abating a bit now. I should think everything ought to be all right until the morning. Thanks for the tea, Mrs. Lawrence!'

He saluted them both briskly and strode towards his striped car. Sherry took a step after him, startled.

'I'm not . . .' she began.

Dee reached out a hand and checked her.

'I shouldn't,' he advised quietly.

'Shouldn't what?'

'Tell him you're not Mrs. Lawrence,' Dee retorted, and his voice sounded amused. 'You've just told him we're going home, remember? If you tell him now you're not Mrs. Lawrence, whatever will he think?'

CHAPTER THREE

THE van was blessedly dark inside. Dee held the door open for her and Sherry climbed in, averting her hot face, thankful that he made no move to help her ascend. As soon as she was safely inside the door slammed shut, and she settled back in her seat, glad that it was the bucket and not the bench type, so that she could sit divorced from the driver. Automatically she felt around for a seat belt.

'It's fixed to the pillar beside you.'

Dee slid in next to her and shut his door with a bang. Seeing her fumbling in the dark, he turned to help. 'Press the knob and pull,' he directed, then when she still fumbled, 'let me, your fingers are too frozen.'

'No, I can manage.' To her relief the catch gave, and Sherry slipped inside the belt. For the second time that day she did not want Dee to notice that her fingers trembled, and it was not entirely from the cold. Despite the arctic temperature, her cheeks felt hot.

He was silent on the drive home. Once she made to direct him, but his strong hands were already turning the wheel in the direction she would have indicated.

'I know the way.'

His voice was remote, abstracted, more the voice she was used to, and she settled back respecting his desire to have no distraction while he drove. The porch light made a welcome beam in the darkness as they turned eventually into the entrance to Arne Cottage. Sherry jumped down as Dee pulled to a halt in the wide drive, and stuck her head back through the door.

'Stay where you are and I'll open the garage for you. You can drive straight in.'

He signalled acknowledgment, and she slammed the door shut and headed for the double, studded doors adjacent to the house. She pulled them both wide and signalled Dee in, backing against a privet bush out of the way of the glare of his headlights. He pulled up with ample room to spare, hoisted his suitcase out of the back, and followed Sherry up the porch steps. The front door of the house stood invitingly open, and an appetising smell wafted through. She sniffed appreciatively. It was Polly's way of welcoming them home. Humphrey Manders' housekeeper might present a stern exterior to the world generally, but her heart was in the right place.

'We're home, Polly!' she called, slipping off her coat and rummaging in the hall cupboard for a coat-hanger for Dee. He shrugged out of his mac and handed the filled hanger back to Sherry with a word of thanks, and they both turned as Polly appeared from a door at the end of the hall.

'Another half hour and your dinner would have been spoilt.' She regarded them both grimly.

'We've only just managed to clear up the mess.' Sherry was used to Polly, but Dee looked taken aback. Polly had that effect on most people when they met her for the first time. Her straight, dark stare, which had a way of always seeming disapproving, under the old-fashioned, screwed-back bun that bristled with large black hairpins – despite her years, Polly's hair was of a darkness that no one ever dared to question – and her habit of dressing in unrelieved black, gave her a formidable appearance that was accentuated by her skeletal frame and unusual height. Altogether, Polly was a presence.

'Practically half the roof of Beacon Hire blew right off,' Sherry enlarged, knowing that Polly would not stoop to satisfy her curiosity by questions.

'Roofs can be mended, and you said no one was hurt.'

Polly did not believe in outspoken sympathy, either, but her face softened as she looked at Dee. Relaxed now in the shelter of the comfortable hall, his own looked bleak, and Sherry prayed that the weather would remain dry. At least the damage was reparable so long as the exposed rooms were not subjected to a wetting.

'Come along with me, Mr. Lawrence, I'll show you to your room,' commanded Polly, and turned towards the stairs with a parting shot to Sherry. 'Get your hands washed for dinner, Miss Sherry. I'll be serving it up in about twenty minutes.'

She had said the same thing to Sherry, with variations, for the past twenty odd years, and Dee looked startled, then his expression relaxed in a grin. It made his face look a lot younger, and Sherry smiled back, mentally kicking Polly for speaking to her in front of him as if she was still five years old. Nevertheless, she mounted to her own room obediently, glad to get out of her working attire of trouser suit and motoring coat, and into something more feminine. She took longer than usual over her choice of clothes this evening. It was not because Dee was there, she told herself firmly. Or perhaps it was. She had not wanted to invite him home, but under the circumstances there was little else she could have done, and she wanted to look her best, to impress upon him that she was mistress of herself and her home, and more than capable of running these, and her uncle's business, without any interference from him. It would not help if Polly insisted on treating her as a child. She would have a tactful word with her later, and hope she would co-operate, though it was doubtful if she would. Polly would see no reason to change her ways for a chance guest, and as for trying to impress Dee, Sherry knew that she would not hold with that sort of nonsense, which was her usual expression for other people's behaviour. Eventually she chose a cream wool dress. It was starkly plain, but beautifully cut and had been a birthday present from her uncle. She opened her jewel case and fingered through the contents, finally selecting a tiny, carved brooch made from wood, a bar in the shape of a slender twig supported a cluster of miniature fir cones that swung loosely on delicate gold chains. It complemented the dress, and Sherry ran downstairs feeling that she had done her best. Dee was already in the dining-room when she got there, standing with his hands thrust into his trousers pockets in front of the big log fire. His shoulders had a hunched, despondent look about them, which was not surprising considering what it would cost him to repair his property. Sherry hoped that he was adequately insured.

He straightened as she came in, his hands going out to grasp the back of her chair. With automatic courtesy he pulled it away from the table, waiting for her to sit down before he took out his own opposite to her. Polly had only pulled out one leaf from the table, so that the small expanse of set cloth had a cosy, intimate look, and she had put it close to the fire with the thoughtfulness that Sherry was accustomed to, but never failed to appreciate. Both she and Dee were frozen to the bone, and the steady glow from the scented apple logs penetrated her numbed limbs as even a hot shower had not been able to do. She felt herself relax, and with the ease of tension from the cold a drowsiness began to claim her towards the end of the meal that even the coffee afterwards did little to dissipate.

Replete with Polly's excellent cooking, she lay back in her uncle's wing chair, her hair bright against the dark hide. Dee sat in the chair that was normally hers, his wiry length filling it more adequately than Sherry could. She was glad he had not sat in the hide chair. She had given him the opportunity, allowing him to choose his own seat after the meal was finished, but with a nicety of feeling for which she was grateful he had regarded the two chairs, one on each side of the hearth, with a considering look, and chosen the obviously more feminine one, its smaller dimensions and soft green cloth upholstery indicating its usual occupier as surely as the rich leather covering of the other told of Humphrey Manders' favourite seat beside the double pipe rack fixed against the wall.

Dee settled opposite to her, sipping his coffee, his eyes upon her face. Her delicate bone structure looked almost ethereal in the flickering light and shadow from the hissing logs. Sherry stirred under his gaze, and her slight movement broke the silence between them. They both spoke at once.

'Would you—'

'Your brooch—'

They stopped, and Sherry laughed and held out her hand for his cup.

'I'll give you a refill if you tell me what you were going to say.' Anything, she thought with a kind of desperation, to get some sort of conversation going between them. Now she had brought Dee home she did

44.

not quite know what to do with him, and wished more fervently than ever that her uncle was here to cope for her. When she had given her impulsive invitation she had not thought of the fact that as a guest she would have to keep him company in the long evenings after dinner, and entertain a man who until this afternoon had been a stranger to her in every respect that mattered. A casual business acquaintance was no help in getting to know the real person behind the impersonal working front of everyday, and there was the week-end to get through as well. Sherry's mind balked. Time enough, she decided, to worry about that when it arrived. Maybe by then the roof of Dee's premises would have been repaired, she thought hopefully, and he would be back in his own flat. The possibility gave her heart, and she poured him an extra generous measure of cream in his coffee on the strength of it.

'Whoa!' His protest stayed her hand.

'Sorry! I forgot you said you liked it strong,' she apologized, hesitating with the cup in her hand.

'As it rises will do,' he smiled taking it from her, 'and I was about to inquire where your brooch came from. It's very effective on that dress, and most unusual.'

Sherry gave him a startled look. She would not have suspected the erstwhile brisk, businesslike owner of Beacon Hire of noticing a small item like a brooch, let alone whether or not it looked good against her dress.

'It comes from Norway.' Surprised into response, she unclipped the wooden twig and handed it to him. 'It's hand-carved.'

'So I see.' He turned the tiny carving in his fingers, appreciating the delicate craftsmanship of the ornament fashioned from formless wood by unknown hands. His own were slender and brown, the fingers long, ending in close-cut filbert nails. The hands of an artist, and despite his mechanically based trade, well cared for.

'It needs a cross bill perched on the top,' he smiled, handing it back to her carefully.

'A – what?'

'A crossbill. A sort of finch,' he explained. 'Somewhere along the line the ends of its beak got crossed one over the other.' He crossed the tips of two fingers to show her. 'That's how it got its name. They like eating the seeds of fir cones.' He tapped the tiny carved cones with a gentle finger, setting them swinging as if the bird he spoke about had just taken wing and quit the twig, with only the tremble of the cones left to tell of its passing.

'You're interested in birds,' remarked Sherry, thinking of the sketches on the walls of his living room.

'In the feathered variety,' he retorted, his lips lifting, and a flicker of laughter dancing in his blue gaze. His smile widened as he watched Sherry's colour rise, and she stiffened with the now familiar vexation that this man should have the power to disconcert her. She supposed it stemmed from her resentment that he had been asked to keep an eye on Manders Motors while her uncle was away, and she determined that she would not let it show in her attitude to him while he was at Arne Cottage. He had come here at her invitation, and at all costs she must not let him suspect that she regretted it.

'You won't forget Miss Lomax is coming at eight o'clock, Miss Sherry?'

Polly appeared silently through the door, her soft shoes giving out no sound on the thick carpet, and her funereal clothing making her seem to materialize from the shadows rather than enter the room like a living person. Sherry chuckled to herself as she saw Dee start, then chided herself for being uncharitable. She must not forget that he was her guest, even though he was an undesirable one from her point of view.

'Elizabeth!' she exclaimed. 'I'd forgotten her, and it's nearly eight already.'

'It's just striking,' confirmed Polly as the voice of the grandfather clock in the hall spoke loudly in the quiet house. The echo had hardly died away when there was a crunch of tyres on the gravel sweep outside, a brief flare of headlights crossed the drawn curtains, and the note of a car engine cut into silence. A door slammed, and seconds later a peal on the doorbell announced the arrival of a visitor. Polly grasped the tray of coffee things and hurried to the door. 'I'll let her in,' she told them, closing it behind her.

'Do you know Elizabeth Lomax?' Again her ignorance of Dee as a person struck Sherry forcefully. She did not even know who his friends were. She had never seen him among her own particular circle, at the dances or parties they held, or at the local tennis club. Apart from sketching, and birds, she did not know where his interests lay. If she had even thought of it at all, she would have assumed his life consisted of his business and practically nothing else. Although the social life of Beacon Downs was varied, it was small enough for those who participated to bump into one another at some time or another during the year, and she had never bumped into Dee. Her companion shook his head.

'You mean Hereward Lomax's daughter, I take it?' Sherry nodded. 'I haven't met her, but I know of her, of course. Who in Beacon Downs doesn't?'

Not many, Sherry supposed. Elizabeth's father owned what must be the largest business in the area, a thriving component firm with a high proportion of export orders that brought buyers from all parts of the world to the small Border town, so that it no longer caused even a raised eyebrow at the Royal Hotel to have guests from the Arab world one week, and the near-Arctic the next. That was where Elizabeth was so useful to her father. Like Sherry, she had elected to earn her own living when she left school, and had turned her natural gift for languages to a good account as an interpreter. To Sherry's knowledge she spoke four tongues fluently, and could get by with two more, which helped with almost every client except the Chinese, she confessed once ruefully, allowing herself to admit defeat in that one, incomprehensible tongue.

'I'll clear off and leave you to your tête-à-tête,' said Dee, rising from his chair.

'No, stay and meet Elizabeth.' Impulsively Sherry put her hand on his sleeve, detaining him by her side. Her friend could help her entertain her unwanted guest, she decided. Liz was more used than she was to coping with strangers, and to all intents and purposes Dee was a stranger to her. She felt her own fund of small talk was rapidly running out. 'We shan't embarrass you with girlish confidences,' she assured him.

'Not tonight, we shan't.' Elizabeth walked through the door, turning to smile at Polly. 'Thanks, Polly, we'll let ourselves in.' The close friendship that had started between Elizabeth and Sherry when they were at school had made Arne Cottage as open, and as familiar, to Hereward Lomax's daughter as her parents' more imposing home, Lomax House, on the other side of the town. 'This way, Andy' she called, and a burly figure followed her through the door, ducking his head under the lintel as he came through. 'Mother was nervous of me driving after the storm,' she explained, 'although the wind seemed to have practically died out before we started, but you know how she frets, so Andy offered to bring me along.'

'Hope you don't mind, Miss Manders?'

'Of course not.' Sherry took his proffered hand thankfully. Andy Vaughan was a bonus. Elizabeth would have helped her out well enough with entertaining Dee, but another man for him to talk to was even better, and the friendliness of the Canadian business-man would melt any social stiffness. 'Come and sit down,' she invited him, 'and call me Sherry, not Miss Manders.'

'I guess we know one another well enough by now,' he acknowledged with a slow smile. Sherry had met him once or twice at Lomax House when Elizabeth's father had been entertaining business guests, and she had been roped in by her friend as an extra lady.

'The trouble with business entertaining, at least in our line of country, is that they're all men,' Elizabeth often complained. 'If only they'd bring their wives with them, it would make things a lot easier.'

'Then there'd be nothing for the women to do during the day while their menfolk were haggling,' Sherry pointed out reasonably, and her friend laughed.

'I suppose not, and then I'd be complaining about having to entertain all women,' she admitted. 'Andy Vaughan hasn't even got a wife, so we feel even more obliged to look after him,' she had grumbled the first time he came over as representative of the Toronto

49

branch of his firm, but Sherry had detected no signs of dissatisfaction from Elizabeth on his second and subsequent visits, indeed he seemed to be in England – and in Elizabeth's company – more during the past few months than he was in Canada.

'He seems partial to Beacon Downs,' she commented slyly after his fourth trip across.

'I think he is.' Elizabeth's fair skin took on a rosy tinge. 'I think I could get to like Canada,' she confessed with a twinkle, and Sherry squeezed her arm affectionately.

'Don't keep me in the dark,' she commanded, and her friend promised.

'I won't. But there's nothing to tell, yet.'

That had been during the autumn, and now he was in England again, and was presumably going to stay over Christmas. If Andy did marry Elizabeth, thought Sherry, he would be a very lucky man. She watched her friend as she came towards them across the spacious room. As always, Sherry was impressed by her graceful carriage, indicative of early ballet training, and a love of walking the open downland that surrounded her home town. Her deep, honey-coloured hair, innocent of curl, was coiled loosely back from her face in a careless knot, showing to advantage her high cheekbones that still held the warm bronze of her recent business trip to the Mediterranean countries with her father.

'I'm begging help for our children's party on Boxing Day,' she confessed, 'but it will do another time if I'm interrupting?' Her questioning glance went from Sherry to Dee, and it held a laughing query that Sherry wanted to deny hotly. She would, when she had Elizabeth on her own, but she could not say anything now, least of all in front of Dee.

'You're not,' was the most she could go to, and her voice held the fervour of determination not to let her visitors go now they were here. 'Dee has come to stay with us for a while until his roof is repaired.' Her momentary confusion made her slightly inarticulate as she performed the necessary introductions, and Dee took pity on Elizabeth's puzzled look, and provided a more comprehensive explanation.

'Goodness what rotten luck!' she exclaimed. 'It must have been practically the last bad gust, too. The wind has died down quite a lot, otherwise I wouldn't have ventured out tonight, not even with Andy driving.' She looked contrite. 'Actually, I could do with help from you both, but this hardly seems the time to ask for it.'

'Go ahead,' Dee invited. 'There's no irreparable damage done at my place, it looks like structural damage only, and we shall get repairs going as soon as it's light in the morning. I'm hoping to beg temporary space in Sherry's office as well as in her home,' he admitted, with a questioning look in the direction of his hostess.

'Naturally you'll share our office,' replied Sherry calmly, her cool tone giving no indication of the exasperation that welled up inside her at the thought of Dee being actually on the premises of Manders Motors during the day, as well as being nominally in charge. She had known that she must offer him working space there, but she had thrust the thought of it from her until now, hating the idea of his company during working hours as well as in her free time.

The sooner he gets his roof mended and returns to his own premises the better, she decided grimly, or there might easily be a break in diplomatic relations between the two businesses before her uncle returned home.

'Do you mean the children's party your firm gives every year?'

She steered the conversation on to safer ground, fearing her treacherous colour might betray her feelings. That was the worst of being auburn-haired, the fine skin that went with it acted like a barometer to the owner's emotions.

'That's the one,' her friend nodded, 'only this year we're stuck for transport. When we decided to get rid of our own vehicles and put all our transport requirements out to contract starting in the New Year, we forgot the party. But of course you both know all about this,' she went on, 'our inquiries for tender for the contract have already been sent out to you and Mr. Lawrence, as well as to Saville Hire,' she mentioned the only other transport business in Beacon Downs.

'Dee,' commanded Dee quietly, and Elizabeth gave him a swift smile.

'Christiain names make things easier,' she allowed in her easy-going way which Sherry had always envied her.

'We haven't had any inquiry from your firm, Liz. This is the first I've heard of your change of plans at the works. When was it sent out?' asked Sherry.

It would be a wonderful feather in her cap if she could land a long-term contract for the garage while her uncle was away. It would prove that she could not only keep the place ticking over, but take positive action on her own responsibility to get new business. She knew that where Lomax was concerned she would be on the same footing as any other contestant for the job. Not Dee, of course, he would be after the goods transport side, which didn't interest Manders Motors, but she still had Saville Hire to contend with, and they were a formidable rival, being a bigger firm than her uncle's. Her friendship with Elizabeh would make no difference, she would not want it to, and they had always kept their personal lives and business relationships strictly apart by a kind of unspoken agreement that had worked very well on both sides.

'It was posted about a week ago,' returned her friend, 'it should have reached you by now.'

'It's the Christmas post, I expect,' said Sherry. 'I've noticed the mail seems to be anyhow these last few days.'

'We must both be suffering from the same postman,' Dee broke in. 'I haven't had your contract either.'

'Not to worry.' Elizabeth took business difficulties in her stride. 'Your premises are opposite to one another, so it could be that a delivery has gone astray. I know Saville Hire have had theirs, I saw one of their men at the Royal this morning when I was checking on some rooms we had booked for a couple of foreign V.I.P.s who are coming to tour the works, and he mentioned it then.

'Does that mean we're too late to put in a quote?' Dee's voice was brisk and businesslike.

'No, since you two haven't had your inquiries I'll have copies sent out for you and put the decision off until the next Board Meeting,' replied Elizabeth. 'Will the damage to your premises make for any difficulty in fulfilling a contract for the time being?' Elizabeth's voice was as practical as Dee's.

'None at all,' he returned promptly, in a confident tone. 'None of my vehicles was touched, fortunately. As I said, it's purely structural damage, and that's only a matter of getting a new roof on. It's nuisance value only so far as the business itself is concerned, and in no way disabling.'

If Dee could get the contract, it would help to pay for the cost of the damage, thought Sherry, and knew a swift hope that he would be successful, although he didn't sound particularly worried about the cost, doubtless he had got it well insured, most people in the town took out policies against storm damage, since it was high-sited and prone to gale force winds which usually took their toll of the local chimney stacks every winter. Nevertheless it was a relief to know that Beacon Hire would be all right; she would not have liked to see any business founder that had had so much hard work put into it as Dee's to bring it to its present state of prosperity.

'I was going to ask Saville Hire to quote for a coach for the party as well, but I forgot,' confessed Elizabeth, and Sherry rounded on her friend wide-eyed.

'Pay for a coach for the children's party? You can have one from us free, for that.' Once more she knew what her uncle would have done, only this time she did it with no personal reservations.

'You can have one of my vans for any hauling you need done, as well,' said Dee forthrightly.

They both knew of the Lomax Company's children's party, which rounded up every able-bodied child in the district on Boxing Day, including those from the local children's home, and gave them the time of their small lives, and a generous present to go home with. For the unlucky ones confined in hospital, and the few outside who could not come for one reason or another, there was a visit from Father Christmas and an extra generous present in compensation. It was Hereward Lomax's way of giving back to the town that had nurtured his business, and although a good half of its prosperity now came from foreign trade, the party was one event on its business calendar that was regarded as a must by everyone at the firm. Faced with such a request, both Sherry and Dee responded instantly and willingly.

'Actually we could do with a lorry to haul the Christmas tree.'

'Count a lorry and a van,' said Dee promptly, and Elizabeth's smile brightened.

'I'm very glad I came tonight, in spite of the storm. Dad will be delighted,' she assured them.

She rose to go, refusing the offer of supper, and Andy Vaughan rose with her.

'We mustn't stay late. Mother worries, and after the storm today she will fret even though I've got a chauffeur,' she smiled. She turned an inquring look on Sherry. 'Why don't you bring Dee along to the party with you this year?' she asked. 'Sherry usually drops in to help us at teatime on Boxing Day,' she explained to Dee, 'and as you're staying with her ... Andy's coming, but we could always do with more help, that is if you don't mind jammy fingers?'

Sherry caught her breath. Surely Dee wouldn't still be at Arne Cottage at Christmas? The idea was unthinkable. Roofs couldn't possibly take so long to repair. She opened her mouth to tell Elizabeth, but Dee forestalled her.

'I'd be delighted,' he assured the fair-haired girl smilingly, 'and I don't mind jammy fingers in the least,' he added.

CHAPTER FOUR

SHERRY woke the next morning with the feeling that something was different. The sound of out-of-tune whistling from the bathroom reminded her of what it was, and she pulled a brush through her hair with quick, impatient strokes.

It was not yet light outside, the tardy dawn of midwinter slow to reveal the whereabouts of the playthings of yesterday's gale. She was eager for breakfast to be over, so that she could get back to the garage and see for herself how bad the damage was to Dee's premises. Maybe, she thought hopefully, it had looked worse than it really was, last night.

When Dee decanted her from the van on to the garage pull-in an hour later, one glance told her that her optimism was unjustified. Daylight made the gale-torn second storey look even worse, if anything, than it had the night before. Mercifully the single-storey workshops had not been damaged, but the office area and Dee's flat looked as if a bomb had hit it. Dee gave a groan as he surveyed his wrecked property.

'What a mess! It only needs a blizzard now . . .'

'Don't invite one!' Sherry's tone was sharp. Some of Polly's superstition must have rubbed off on her, for she crossed her fingers hastily.

A grin showed briefly on Dee's set face.

'Thanks for trying,' he indicated her fingers, 'but we can only hope for the best. You go in out of the wind, and I'll join you later – that is if it's still O.K. for me to share your office?'

'Of course it is.' Conscience made Sherry's tone heartier than it might otherwise have been. 'But what about your phones?'

'Do you think you could ring the engineers for me, and ask if there's anything they can do about rigging up a line from my number into your office?' asked Dee. 'The phones are going to be the only real problem so far as I can see. I can lock away any paperwork over there and deal with my post and so on from your office.'

'He sounds as if he has got everything nicely organized,' thought Sherry, and stifled a prick of resentment. She would not have thought much of him had he sat down and complained about his evil luck, so it was not fair to criticize him for facing up to the problem and getting it remedied. She fished in her pocket for the office key. 'I'll ring the G.P.O. right away,' she promised, 'with a bit of luck they'll be able to run a temporary line across.'

That, in fact, was what they did. With commendable helpfulness in view of the extra load of work the gale had caused them, they fixed it so that Dee's number rang on a spare instrument in the room that she and her uncle shared as an office. Sherry left the engineers to it, busy at her own desk with the morning post and the dozen and one odds and ends that accumulate in a hectic line of business, and she did not notice until they had gone that they had left the phone on her uncle's desk, on a piece of cable that was too short for it to be put anywhere else. She tried not to look at it as Dee came into the room, but the extra phone drew her eyes like a magnet.

'That was quick work,' approved Dee, indicating the instrument. 'Thanks for coping.' He paused, watching her traitorous colour rise and fall, then he deliberately reached out a long foot and hooked it under the staff of the spare wooden chair under the window. Drawing it to him, he ignored Humphrey Manders' swivel chair, and perched himself on the plain wooden seat, using the back of the big desk where it jutted out as a table overhang for visitors. 'This will do me fine,' he remarked casually. 'With a bit of luck I shan't have to bother you for long. I'll phone round and see what can be done about getting a temporary cover on the roof at least.'

At the end of a frustrating half hour on the phone, it appeared that his luck was not holding. The gale had done a considerable amount of damage in the town, and Beacon Hire was towards the end of a long queue of properties all requiring similar attention. Dee ran desperate fingers through his hair and turned an exasperated face in Sherry's direction.

'The most any of them can promise is to lash some tarpaulins across the roof to keep out the wet, and start on repair work in a week or two,' he exploded. 'The only definite promise I've had is early in the New Year, and I've rung eight building firms already,' he told her incredulously.

'In that case you'll just have to accept the earliest quote,' said Sherry, deliberately keeping her voice practical, but her heart sank. Elizabeth's assumption that Dee would still be with her on Boxing Day had been justified. Christmas at Arne Cottage would be quiet anyway this year, with Humphrey Manders away, but she felt she would have preferred to spend the day in front of the fire with Polly rather than entertain a stranger. Her conscience reminded her that it was the season of goodwill, and she sat upon it firmly. There was a limit.

'Maybe I'd better fix a room at the Royal,' Dee's voice broke in on her thoughts, and she started guiltily as if he had read them.

'Don't be silly!' she snapped, then amended her tone hurriedly. 'If you'd prefer to be at the Royal over Christmas that's up to you, of course. I've no doubt it will be livelier there.' Dee might after all prefer what Christmas gaiety the hotel could offer, rather than remain at Arne Cottage with only herself and Polly for company. She hadn't thought of that. And now she did think of it, she found she did not much like the idea. 'Polly always said I was contrary,' she reminded herself wryly, but it stood to reason that they would miss her uncle's company, and Dee might be better than facing a depleted household for the first time that she could remember at Christmas. 'If you want to book in there, go ahead,' she told him indifferently, 'but you'll have to tell Polly what arrangements you've made. I'm not going to,' she decided firmly.

'Hmmmm ...' The thought of Polly brought Dee up abruptly, and his hand came away from the phone with more haste than dignity. Sherry gave a gurgle of amusement.

'Polly's all right when you get to know her,' she defended the housekeeper.

'She scares me,' admitted Dee, an embarrassed grin spreading across his features. 'I feel like a naughty six-year-old.'

Sherry laughed outright. 'That's probably how you look, to Polly,' she told him callously, 'but her heart's in the right place,' she assured him. 'If she likes you, she'll do practically anything for you. And she must like you,' she added.

'How do you know?' He sounded dubious.

'Because she packed you up a piece of her special gingerbread for your elevenses,' Sherry told him, unwrapping her own as the daily help appeared at the door with a steaming up of tea. 'Can we have two, now, please, Daisy? Mr. Lawrence is camping out with us until his own place has been repaired.' She took a second mug from the tray and put it into Dee's outstretched hand. 'If Polly didn't like you, you would have had plain biscuits in your packet, or no packet at all,' she informed him gravely. 'Gingerbread with real ginger in it is Polly's speciality.' She bit into her own piece, relishing the sharp bite of the preserve on her tongue. 'Polly only gives it to people she approves of. Drat that phone!' She licked the last crumb hastily from her fingers, and picked up the receiver. 'Yes, I'll be right along. In under the hour . . . a passenger from the airport,' she enlightened Dee, dropping the receiver back on its rest. She reached for her coat and made for the door with hasty steps.

'Leave the door for me,' called Dee as she moved to shut it behind her on the way out. 'I can see the Panda driver at the gate, he might be looking for me.' He followed her out, still eating through the generous dark slice in his hand.

'Morning, ma'am.' The young officer of the night before saluted briskly, and Sherry regarded him with amazement.

'Goodness, don't you ever sleep? You were on duty last night.'

'I'd just come on, then. And now I'm just going off,' he grinned. 'We've all had to do an hour or so extra, the storm caused all sorts of damage last night,' he explained. 'I just thought I'd make a last check here before I handed over to the day man.'

'Thoughtful of you', approved Dee, 'but as you see we've got nearly all the railings straightened. I had the men start on them as soon as they came in this morning, and it's only a matter of bolting them back into place now.' He indicated the busy team of workmen intent on their task, and the policeman nodded.

'You should be all right security-wise by dark, then. That will be one worry less for us.'

'I suppose you don't know if there are any road blocks on the way to the airport?' inquired Sherry, suddenly turning back with her hand on the handle of the car door. If there were any diversions the policeman would probably know where they were, and it might save her holdups on the journey.

'None that I've heard of,' returned the officer cheerfully. 'Why are you off on holiday for Christmas?'

'No such luck,' mourned Sherry.' I'm only going to collect a passenger off the Paris flight. It's a regular run for us,' she explained.

The policeman regarded her consideringly.

'I didn't know you did any of the driving yourself, Mrs. Lawrence,' he remarked, with a faint note of disapproval in his voice. 'Couldn't you leave the trips to the chauffeurs during the bad weather? There was a lot of black ice on the road across the downs this morning.'

'There he goes again!' thought Sherry, feeling her ready colour rise. She risked a fleeting glance at Dee, and scowled at his twitching lips. 'I'm as capable of driving as the men – and I'm not Mrs. Lawrence,' she snapped, and ducked hastily into the car to hide her burning face, which was more indignation than confusion now. How dared he criticize her driving – and as

61

for calling her Mrs. Lawrence, let Dee do the explaining, she thought with exasperation. He had got her into it – she knew that was not really fair, but she felt unrepentant – so he could get her out of it. The joke had gone quite far enough. And it was no business of the police who did the driving; she might be small in stature, but she was quite capable of handling her car, even though it was a big one, and was more than capable of deciding when to take the vehicle herself or send one of the drivers, she thought with a toss of her head.

She turned cautiously into the road, conscious of the eyes of the two men following her. They seemed to bore into her back and it made her extra careful. It would be just her luck now to do something awful and get booked, particularly with Dee looking on. But nothing happened. She tried the brake pedal experimentally, and it held. Ben must have been up very early to get it mended, she thought gratefully. She had not seen him that morning, but Paul the apprentice had told her that her car was ready for the road, which meant in Ben's parlance that it was as perfect as he could make it.

Concentrating on her task, she forgot her indignation, and was conscious only of a growing feeling of dismay as she wound her way through the town and saw evidence in almost every street of damage caused by the wind the day before. No wonder Dee had had difficulty in finding a builder to start repairing his roof straight away. At this rate it would take weeks for the local contractors to cope with the amount of damage, and if Dee was at the end of the queue it would probably mean he would be staying at Arne Cottage until well into the New Year. Beacon Downs was used to wind storms, but this was exceptional even for them, and Sherry realized with a sinking feeling in the pit of her stomach that she must either put up with Dee's company at work and at home on a fairly long-term basis, or openly turn him out. She did not find the thought pleasant as she took the fork that pointed her away from the West Gate and on to the main road via a back way through the town. She had no intention of risking another trip across the trench, and further incurring her unwelcome guest's disapproval.

During the night the wind had veered due east, and dropped to a thin, penetrating knife, which probably accounted for the fact that there had been ice on the roads during the early hours. Its force now hardly stirred the trees, and once on the open road beyond Battle Pools, now still grey mirrors on either side of the bridge, the silence of the downs was almost uncanny after the blustering din of the day before. What ice there had been had melted, and the going was good. The car engine took on a high, contented purr that is music in the ears of any driver, and it seemed no time before Sherry was back at the desk in the terminal building inquiring for her passenger. The lounge was not very full, but it would quickly get busy again, she knew, once normal flights were operating. The flying field had been accepting incoming planes for the past hour or so, and the outgoing flights were almost back to normal, so the desk clerk informed her.

'There's your passenger, Miss Manders,' he indicated a man in a dark business suit, carrying a briefcase. 'He's for the Lomax works, but he wants to go to the Royal and drop his things first.'

'The car's outside.' She smiled at her passenger, establishing contact, and somehow managed to hide her chagrin when he expressed surprise that his chauffeur was a girl. Why was it that nine men out of ten thought women were incapable of doing anything but boiling potatoes? she thought furiously, and felt a savage sympathy for members of the Women's Lib movement, which up until now she had always faintly despised. And she didn't like dark-haired men who greased their hair flat, she decided sourly, catching a glimpse of her passenger as she twisted in her seat to back the car out of the way of someone who had parked perilously close to her near side. It looks like black plastic, she thought with a quirk of amusement, then 'Poor Elizabeth'. She compared her passenger's impeccable grooming unfavourably with Dee's curly fairness, that had seemed since she got to know him better over the last few days to be in a constant state of disarray through his habit of running his hands through his hair whenever anything bothered him. He had had a lot to bother him during the past twenty-four hours, Sherry acknowledged fairly, then shook herself impatiently. She did not want to think about Dee and his problems. They had also become her problems, in a way she did not welcome, and she would be heartily thankful when things were back to normal. When Dee solved his difficulties, it would automatically solve hers, she thought thankfully, and by that time her uncle should be nearly due back as well.

In a mood of exasperation at circumstances that were not of her making, and over which she seemed to have no real control, she swung the car clear and pointed its nose back towards Beacon Downs. As she crossed the bridge over Battle Pools she saw the diversion sign was firmly on its feet, and obediently she followed the direction of the arrow, turning through the next breach in the town wall and mentally adjusting her route to come to the Royal from the opposite direction.

There was a good deal of storm damage at this end of the town, which was more exposed than the other. Several quite large pieces of masonry had evidently hit the streets from a height at some time during the storm, and she could see the flashing lights of a couple of police vehicles far ahead of her along the street. She clicked her tongue impatiently. There was no way of avoiding the hold-up, she was in a one-way street so she could not turn, and she settled patiently into her seat to await her turn in the queue. She crawled to a halt behind a couple of Minis, and could see over the tops of their roofs the figure of a policeman wending his way along the line of stationary vehicles, ducking to speak to each driver in turn. Sherry wound her window down ready to take his directions.

'Having trouble?' she inquiried facetiously.

'I'll say!' he retorted fervently. 'A demolition contractor started in on that old warehouse at the top of the street yesterday, and the wind last night decided to help him along. It blew part of a wall over, and the rest of it's liable to topple at any minute. You'll have to take the next turn right, and go round, the whole of the street is cordoned off from there. It won't delay your passenger more than a few minutes,' he nodded politely to the man in the rear compartment. He stood away from the car, and waved her on, and Sherry inched her way forward after the other vehicles, thankful when she finally turned in at the Royal and handed her passenger and his luggage into the care of the porter.

'What a mess!' she exclaimed. 'There are bricks and

mortar all over the place, and a hold-up in the middle of the town that would take a bulldozer to move. It looks like being traffic jams and delays every time we have to come through the town centre for the next day or so,' she grumbled resignedly.

'Then come along with us where there isn't any traffic, and give your nerves a break.' Elizabeth appeared at her elbow and buttonholed her gaily. 'I could do with your help.'

'You've just had it,' retorted Sherry. 'I've brought you a customer.'

'I know, he's joining us for lunch in a few minutes, but there's time for us to talk first,' said her friend hurriedly. 'The Council have told us we can choose a Christmas tree this year from the conifer plantation by the side of Battle Pools. We could do with a man's help really, to choose the right tree, I've got simply no idea of height and so on,' she confessed. 'I thought it would be a good idea if you could get Dee to come with us. He will have to handle the tree as he's providing the lorry for it,' she said reasonably, 'and I thought if we all went to the plantation on Sunday we should be able to choose something between us that's suitable for our party and his lorry at the same time.'

'I'd love to. Anything to go somewhere quiet,' Sherry responded fervently. 'Is Andy coming too?'

'No, he's not, he's here on business, in case you might have forgotten,' said a cheerful Canadian twang from behind them. 'Remember that contract I'm supposed to be discussing with your father?' he asked Elizabeth. 'We shall never finish our haggling if I keep going out with you,' he smiled. 'O.K., I'll help you to decorate it,' he capitulated, seeing her face drop.

'I wonder if they're going to get engaged,' thought

66

Sherry. Elizabeth hadn't told her any more yet, so Andy couldn't have spoken to her, or if he had Elizabeth hadn't been able to give him an answer. It was easy to see how Andy felt, his feelings were plainly written on his face for even the most unobservant to see, but Elizabeth's feelings were not so obvious. Sherry remembered her laughing remark about getting to like Canada, and wondered anew. Her friend wasn't a person who would give her heart easily, she knew, but once it was surrendered it would be steadfast, and for that reason she would have to be very sure before she finally gave her answer. There could be no half measures with Elizabeth, and Sherry hoped for Andy's sake that her friend would be able to respond to his feelings, though she knew that that would never be until the fair-haired girl was certain beyond any doubt that she could give her heart wholly, and without reservations.

'Don't forget to bring Dee with you,' Elizabeth reminded her as they parted. We don't want to choose a tree that won't fit his lorry.'

'I won't,' promised Sherry, with a fervour that raised her friend's eyebrows inquiringly. Elizabeth was not to know how much she dreaded having to look after Dee during the long, blank space of Sunday afternoon, and having the onus of entertaining him entirely on her own suddenly inadequate-feeling shoulders. If she took him along with them to the conifer plantation she would be relieved of at least some of the responsibility of looking after her unwanted guest, she thought with relief, and wondered depressingly how many more Sunday afternoons she would have to get through in his company before his premises were restored to normal, and she could be free again.

CHAPTER FIVE

THE week-end passed more easily than Sherry had dared to hope. A firm of contractors arrived first thing on the Saturday morning and began lashing tarpaulins on the roofless second storey of Beacon Motors, and Dee spent the entire day helping them, and generally clearing up the mess in his shattered office and living quarters. Sherry could not offer to help him because her time was already fully booked driving wedding cars, and she stifled a prick of conscience that told her she ought not to be glad about this.

The entire fleet of Manders Motors was booked on various weddings in the town for the whole of the day, including two of the coaches which were being used to transport guests to the reception of one particularly big wedding. Sherry herself took the bride and the bridegroom to the airport afterwards.

'We're off on safari,' the bride confided as she inquired if they had more than the two modest suitcases that had already been put in the boot of her car. 'We shall be in bush shirts and slacks for most of the time, so we're not burdening ourselves with unnecessary luggage. We can get anything else we need out there.'

Sherry regarded the exquisitely dressed girl in the expensive fur coat with a surprise she was unable to hide.

'Oh, we shall leave this lot in Nairobi,' the bride said with a careless shrug, and Sherry opened the car door for her wordlessly. A safari was the last choice of honeymoon she would have expected the sophisticated-looking couple to have made. The ski slopes of St. Moritz would have been her guess, from the size of the wedding and the quality of the bride's going-away outfit, but you could never tell with people, she reflected; the most ordinary-looking types often behaved in the most extraordinary ways.

At least with the more luxurious functions, the guests tended to use the more expensive rose-petal type of confetti, she thought, counting her blessings as she surveyed the coloured litter in the passenger compartment later. The bride and groom had shaken themselves as clear as possible in the car before getting out at the airport, and the sober grey upholstery of the back seat had a candy floss gaiety about it that brought a smile to her lips, despite the clearing up it would entail later. The only trouble with paper rose petals was that their very size made them stick in the pipe of the vacuum cleaner more easily than the smaller sort. She sighed resignedly. Thank goodness there was still a brisk wind blowing. It would never do if her next passenger happened to be a blue-suited business type he would not appreciate being covered in confetti on his way to a conference!

She checked in her mirror and saw that she had the road to herself. Within seconds she pulled to a standstill on the frost-hardened turf at the side of the road, and enlisted the aid of the elements. The wind had done enough damage, she thought, it might as well be harnessed to do a bit of good. Following the common practice of the drivers from the garage she parked the big vehicle sideways on to the wind and opened all the doors, letting the keen air blow straight through.

As if they had suddenly come to life, the delicately coloured paper petals danced off the seat and floor and through the far doorway, brightening the winter drab of the bleak hillside with an artificial gaiety reminiscent of the function that she had just left.

'That's one job less for Paul,' she said aloud, shutting the doors on the now spotless vehicle, and shivering a little as she resumed her seat. The wind had taken the rose petals out of it, but had also taken the heat. She reached out and pulled the booster on the dashboard and sat for a while with the engine running, luxuriating in the swift warmth that radiated from the hot engine. Standing in the teeth of the wind on the open downs had made her good wool trouser suit seem as thin as cotton. She thought of the bride she had just left, and the luxurious fur she had accepted so casually. Sherry did not care for the larger weddings much. She preferred the smaller, homelier wedding parties; they seemed more real to her than the big, sophisticated affairs, of massive guest lists and huge receptions.

'All dress and no vows,' was how Polly once put it, and although she had teased the housekeeper then for being old-fashioned, a little, secret corner of her heart agreed with what Polly had said. If ever she got married, she thought, their own parish church would do nicely for her. The Castle Chapel, it was called locally, being all that was left of the once fine church attached to the now ruined fortress. During the last century it had been lovingly restored by hands that revered its ancient beauty, and it still retained a finely carved rood screen, and glorious stained glass windows that had somehow escaped the attentions of the warring armies that centuries ago had spilled across the Border hills, like locusts laying waste whatever crossed their path.

'History's vandals,' her uncle had called them, running angry twentieth-century fingers across the deep scars in the age-darkened wood of the loosebox pews, where mounted soldiers had driven iron rings into them, to be used for tethering points, indifferently using the sacred place to stable their weary mounts. The flow of battle that had scarred the Castle Chapel had not lapped against the walls of the church that topped the hill in the centre of Beacon Downs, which was a much larger building, more impressive and just as ancient, but to Sherry's mind its very size lent it a remoteness that was not a part of her.

By the time evening came both Sherry and Dee were too tired with their day's activities to want more than dinner and an early night in bed, and it was not until Sunday morning that she remembered she had a guest to entertain, and a blank morning to get through. Elizabeth's trip to the conifer plantation at Battle Pools would nicely take care of the afternoon, but there Sherry's mind stopped.

'I usually take Polly to church,' she mentioned tentatively to Dee at breakfast time.

'I'd like to come with you if that's all right with Polly?' Dee had established friendly relations with the housekeeper, but he still sounded wary.

'Anyone who can sing is welcome,' retorted Sherry, hiding her surprise.

Polly seemed to feel none, taking the news of an extra passenger with her usual unruffled calm. She poked a lethal-looking hatpin through her best black felt, disdaining to look in the mirror beside her on the wall, and accepted her spiky umbrella without which she was rarely seen outdoors winter or summer.

'Mr. Lawrence can drive,' she informed them calmly, and took her seat in the front as if she was accustomed to Dee taking the wheel every Sunday. He gave Sherry a pleading look, but she refused to help him out. With a shrug she opened the back door and got in, annoyed that Polly should have relegated her to the back seat. 'Dee can sort it out for himself,' she thought angrily, 'he seems to be taking over here as well as at work.' She knew that was not fair, but she felt too furious to be just, and after hesitating a moment, watching her face, Dee lifted his shoulders helplessly and got into the front alongside Polly. He fumbled for the seat belt, adjusting it to his own needs, and realized that Polly was not doing anything about the one on her side. Sherry had often wondered what the stubborn figure in black would do if wearing seat belts became law. Probably walk, out of sheer awkwardness, she guessed, unless Humphrey Manders could persuade her to conform. So far all his efforts in that direction had been to no avail.

'Let me help you,' smiled Dee, reaching over and unclipping the belt. He slid it gently across the gaunt figure beside him, and Sherry watched open-mouthed. This was something she must tell Uncle Humph when she phoned him tonight. He would not believe her. She could hardly believe it herself, but the evidence was there in front of her own eyes. Polly was safely belted in without even a murmur of protest.

Her temper evaporated under the force of the shock, and she was in a mood more befitting Sunday morning by the time they reached the church and parked in the shelter of the ruins. The familiar ritual of the service calmed her, and unexpectedly she found herself enjoying it, despite her earlier ill humour. They rose for the first hymn. It was a carol, and one of her uncle's favourites, and for a second tears pricked her throat, then Dee's voice rose in a pleasant baritone beside her and she sent hers to join it, losing herself in the joy of singing, their voices in unison with all the others that winged to the roof of the packed little church.

Polly joined them for their midday meal, as she always did on a Sunday, and after helping her to clear away it was time to go and meet Elizabeth.

'Put on something warm,' Dee warned Sherry, 'it can be pretty cold along the path beside Battle Pools. There'll be no shelter until we reach the plantation, and not a lot then, there's very little undergrowth under conifers, and nothing much except the trunks of the trees to stop the wind.'

Sherry looked at him doubtfully. It was all very well for men, they were in trousers and flat-heeled shoes all the time, but today *was* Sunday.

'Never mind what day it is, dress for what we're doing,' Dee commanded. 'It's no good catching cold just to look nice. And anyway, I like to see you in a trouser suit,' he told her.

Sherry raised astonished eyebrows. First the brooch, then this. She had not realized that he ever noticed what she was wearing. Until a few days ago he had only spoken to her and passed on; she might have been one of the men in the garage for all the notice he took of her. Nevertheless, it gave her more choice. Trouser suits were working gear while she was driving, and she had a selection of warm ones that made a neat, workmanlike outfit for the cars, and at the same time allowed her to be fashionable. She chose her newest, in a stout wool weave with a long bush-style jacket and slanting pockets that were ideal for thrusting cold hands into. The cloth was a soft sage green that set off her bright hair, and she teamed it with a chunky white sweater designed to keep out any cold that the December day could produce. She pulled a green and white knitted Fair Isle cap over her curls, its long bobble swinging gaily down over her collar, and picked up a scarf and mittens to match. Her shoes would do. They were tan, flat-heeled slip-ons, that she had worn this morning for church, thinking she had to drive as usual.

They had arranged to meet Elizabeth at the edge of the pools, and her little red runabout pulled to a halt beneath the bridge at the same instant that Dee applied his brakes on the shingle patch at the edge of the water. Elizabeth, too, was in trousers, her hair swinging loose today across her shoulders under a scarlet cap that matched her slacks, her hands already thrust deep into the pockets of her lined mac, out of reach of the searching wind.

'Brrr!' she greeted them. 'Let's get going before we freeze to the spot!'

Suiting action to her words, she strode ahead of them up the path, her lissome tallness making light of the rough track. Dee waited for Sherry to go next, but she waved him on.

'Go ahead, I've got a bit of shingle in my shoe.' She slipped it off and shook out the offending piece of gravel, then, comfortable again, she set off behind the others. They had got several yards' start, and she found to her chagrin that her much shorter legs were no match for theirs. Their tall stride made light of the constant runnels that crisscrossed the path from the pool, straddling them with an ease that Sherry envied. She had to jump, her shorter stride would not reach from bank to bank, and she saw with dismay that the one confronting her was wider than the others, and

74

fairly deep. It had also got a crumbly bank on the other side where someone had obviously had the same trouble. It looked as if they had jumped and missed, and had to scramble up the incline to dry land, and their efforts had left the soil slippery, with an insecure look about it that daunted her. She hesitated on the bank. The others were a yard or two ahead. She opened her mouth to call to them, then shut it abruptly.

'I won't shout for help.' All her native independence rebelled at the idea. If they wanted to forge ahead and leave her to her own devices, let them, she would manage on her own. She stepped back a pace or two and made a run for it, and all would have been well if she had not stepped on a loose stone, right on the edge of the near bank. It rolled under her foot and spoiled her take-off, and she landed with an exclamation of dismay several inches short of firm ground on the other side.

Dee spun round at her cry, and in three long strides he covered the distance between them back to her side. He grabbed her unceremoniously just as the toe of her right shoe slid under the surface of the icy water beneath her, and hoisted her up beside him on to the firmness of the path.

'Has it wet your foot?'

'No, my shoe didn't go in that far.'

'Let me see.'

Keeping one arm about her, he leaned down and lifted her foot. Before she realized what he was about to do he slipped off her shoe and ran inquiring fingers over her sock, feeling to see if the water had penetrated. She curled protesting toes against his touch and tried to wriggle from his grasp, but he held her firmly and with one foot in the air her balance was anything but secure, and she grasped hastily for support at the back of his jacket. Standing on one leg on uneven ground was not the most dignified of positions to be in, and she felt like a naughty two-year-old who had deliberately walked through a puddle just to annoy a grown-up. She half-expected Dee to threaten her with a spanking, but he only replaced her shoe and straightened up, regarding her mutinous face with amused eyes.

'Hang on a minute Liz,' he called out to their companion, 'we're going too fast for Titch here. Walk in front of me so that I can keep my eye on you,' he instructed Sherry. 'Better still, hold my hand.' He reached out for her mitten, but she hastily stuffed her hand into her jacket pocket out of his reach, and hurried on in front of him towards Elizabeth, who waited for her with a mischievous look on her tanned face. So Dee already called her Liz! Considering it was only the second time he had met her he was being pretty familiar, she reflected sourly.

The conifer plantation lay above them, darkly silhouetted against the cold sky. The path rose steeply towards it, away from the edge of the water, and all three of them were warm and panting by the time they reached the first of the tall trunks. Elizabeth leaned her back against the one nearest to her and watched the others struggle up the last few yards of the incline.

'Phew! That was a pull,' gasped Sherry, borrowing part of the trunk beside her friend.

'The path flattens out from here,' consoled Dee, 'and it's easier walking on the pine needles. Watch your step, though,' he warned the two girls, 'this planting is mostly spruce fir, and they're shallow-rooted. They can be toe-catching things if the roots have been uncovered for any reason,' he said feelingly.

'This one looks a bit big for a Christmas tree.' Sherry's eyes travelled doubtfully skyward up the graceful, tapering trunk ending in a delicate spire that seemed almost to reach into the lowering sky. The tiered branches moved gently in the wind, though those further in the plantation remained still, protected on every side by their fellows.

'Goodness! We can't have one this size,' her friend exclaimed. 'Dee would need something a lot bigger than a lorry to carry one of these. There's a newer plantation further on, with younger trees,' she explained. 'They haven't got such a corporation as this chap, and they're not so tall either.' She patted as much of the considerable girth of the trunk as she could reach, and used it as a lever to start her off along the ride that led into the semi-light of the plantation. 'There's a short cut along this ride that brings us on the other side of the hill where the smaller trees are.' She swung along beside Sherry, thoughtfully modifying her longer stride, and Dee did the same on her other side, the wide ride enabling them to walk in comfort three abreast. The faint whine of the wind was muffled here, seeming but a background to the cathedral hush of the great trees. The thick padding of the pine needles underfoot absorbed the sound of their steps, and instinctively the three fell silent themselves, unconsciously offering homage to the primeval mystery of the forest.

Sherry lifted her face, inhaling the tangy spruce scent with relish. It felt good to be outside after spending so much of her time cooped in a car or the office. She turned to Dee, and found him watching her, his vivid blue eyes darkened almost to navy in the dimmed light. He pointed downward without speaking, and

Sherry nodded to let him know she understood. Speech seemed superfluous in this silent place, and she side-stepped to avoid the exposed roots he indicated, catching Elizabeth's arm so that she saw them too, and avoided them in safety.

No one spoke until they breasted the rise and came out of the trees, it seemed suddenly, into full daylight again. A ride twice the width of the one they had just left, with straggling grass coerced by the light to defy the enveloping conifers, made a broad green mat at their feet, separating them from a block planting of similar trees in a much earlier stage of growth. Elizabeth eyed them delightedly.

'They're just what we need. Let's walk through them and pick the very nicest for the party,' she cried enthusiastically. 'Come on, Sherry!'

'Not so fast,' cried Dee. 'You can't just wander in and pick where you like.'

'Why not?' chorused the two girls turning surprised faces to his.

'Women!' he exclaimed. 'I suppose you would walk through the plantation, and nothing would suit you until you got to a tree in the very centre?'

'Probably,' conceded Elizabeth, 'but . . .'

'Why not?' mimicked Dee. 'I'll give you one or two good reasons why not, before you start off,' he said, mock-stern. 'Remember that the tree has got to be felled, then hauled out of the planting with all its branches intact. When they are felled and lopped the hauling is easy, but you don't want smashed branches on a children's Christmas tree. By the way, who have you arranged to fell it for you?'

'Well . . .' Elizabeth hesitated, then caught sight of the glint in his eyes and capitulated. 'No one yet,' she confessed. 'I hadn't even thought of it.'

'The Forestry Commission men will help you there,' Dee relented. 'In fact if you're good, I might even arrange it for you myself,' he offered magnanimously.

'Oh, would you? I should be grateful,' cried Elizabeth, patently relieved.

'What about the other reasons?' prompted Sherry warily. Their Christmas tree for the party looked like being a more complicated acquisition than they had bargained for.

'The other reasons are all my lorry,' retorted Dee. 'Remember it is a four-wheeled, ground-running vehicle, not a helicopter, and it will be a lot easier to load a tree on it if that tree is felled from the outside edge of the plantation. That is, if there's one here that suits madam's choice,' He waved his hand gravely at the solid block of trees entirely clothing the downward slope almost to the edge of the pools in the valley below them.

'Aren't men wet blankets?' grimaced Elizabeth.

'I've got a horrid feeling this one's right,' allowed Sherry grudgingly. A thought struck her. 'I wouldn't like to drive a lorry up this hill, either. Is it safe, d'you think?'

'Perfectly safe if it's handled properly,' replied Dee. 'I'll drive it myself to make sure. And there's a gentler slope coming to this ride from the other direction,' he went on reassuringly, catching the concern on her face. 'It's a longer run, but not nearly so steep, and it makes it a feasible proposition for an ordinary vehicle.'

He seemed to know the layout of the plantations well, and Sherry remembered his love of birdwatching. Probably this was where he came, in which case the hidden, secret corners of the woods would be no secret to him, but warmly familiar, and he would be as much at home here as the birds he liked so well. The feathered variety. Her lips twitched as she remembered his quick riposte, and she coloured as she caught his eyes on her face, a query in his raised brows.

'Let's walk along the ride and choose one from here, then.' She pulled Elizabeth into action hurriedly, turning her back on Dee. 'This one looks about right . . .'

'What about this one? It's a prettier shade of green.'

They chose six in the next three hundred yards, and Dee walked behind them, regarding them with tolerant amusement mixed with male exasperation while they argued the merits of each particular choice. Wide tractor marks in the grass of the ride indicated the activities of foresters, and a pyramid of cut logs confronted them, with one long trunk, uncut on its side on the ground. Sherry flopped to rest on its friendly expanse.

'I'm seeing green!' she wailed. 'All the trees look alike.'

'Why couldn't the Council just give us one, and have done with it?' groaned Elizabeth. 'What're we goin' to do?' she chanted, minstrel style.

'Make Dee choose one,' decided Sherry. 'You said you needed a man's help. Make him earn his keep, and help.'

'At your service!' Dee bowed. 'I wouldn't go shopping with you two if I was paid for the privilege,' he added fervently. 'You must have looked at a couple of hundred trees at least, and not one of them suits,' he marvelled.

'We want one that's special,' protested Elizabeth.

'They're all special.' Dee reached out gentle fingers,

curling them round the soft green needles of the nearest tree, a man at one with his surroundings, revering the life that flowed through the high standing beauty at his side. Sherry saw that he had a long cone in his other hand, there had been a lot among the fallen needles of the ride where they walked. She cocked her head on one side regarding it, and he smiled.

'That's what a jenny wren does.'

'What?' Sherry looked puzzled.

'Never mind. Look, this is where the seeds lie.' Seeing their interest he held it closer for them to examine, and Sherry sighed.

'We used to gather them to put on the fire and make it smell nice, when I was little,' she said wistfully. Cone-gathering expeditions had been fun, with her uncle carrying the roomy basket for their spoils, and even Polly unbending to enjoy the endless games of make-believe, skittles, with big cones set on end under the trees, and hastily gathered smaller cones for ammunition.

'We can gather some to take back now, if you like,' Dee offered. 'After we've chosen the tree, of course,' stopping Elizabeth's protest.

'After *you've* chosen the tree,' chorused the two girls, and he grinned, defeated.

'In that case, if I'm to be allowed the choice we'll walk further down the slope towards the pools,' he decided. 'It won't be such a pull on the vehicle, and the tree will be easier to handle on flatter ground.' He led the way downwards, and the two girls heaved themselves reluctantly to their feet and followed him.

'We can pick up cones on the way,' realized Elizabeth, her enthusiasm returning. 'Look, here's two big ones.' She handed one to Sherry. 'We can put them in our pockets until we get to the car.'

'I suppose so.' Sherry looked doubtful. Her pockets were roomy enough for hands, but seemed unaccountably to shrink when she tried to persuade the portly cone to enter. Its stiff scales caught at the soft woollen cloth, and Dee intervened hastily.

'Not in your suit pocket. Think what Polly would say!' His expression suggested that he didn't want to, and Sherry silently agreed with him. 'Here, wait a minute, you can use this.' He delved into the pocket of his windcheater and brought out a sizeable square scarf that had seen better days. 'Tie the ends together. No, I'll do it,' he decided, tying expertly, and handing the result to Sherry. 'This will hold enough for now, and we can always come cone-gathering again another day if you want to,' he promised, much as he might promise a treat to a favourite niece.

Sherry took it from his hand, feeling again the familiar resentment well up inside her, her quick spirit rebelling at being treated as a child. The upsurge of anger spoilt her pleasure in the cone-gathering, which was a pity, she was just beginning to enjoy the afternoon, in spite of wishing at the start that she and Elizabeth could have been alone as they usually were on their outings together. Quietly she bent and began to fill the makeshift basket. Elizabeth stooped to help her, and Dee strolled on ahead of them, regarding the trees that marched in line beside him downhill with a keen eye.

'We can't get any more in after this one.' Elizabeth topped up the pile of cones in the scarf square, and straightened up, and Sherry grasped the knot at the top and swung it experimentally in her hand. The weight of the cones sank the cloth into a deeper dip until it made an adequate basket for the load it carried, and the two girls started after Dee, who by now was a good distance in front of them down the slope.

'Wait for us,' called Elizabeth. 'I only know the main rides up here,' she confessed to Sherry, 'and not all of them. We don't want to lose sight of Dee and get ourselves lost.'

That would be about the last straw, thought Sherry silently, and she had no doubt that Dee would blame her if they did. She quickened her steps to keep up with the taller girl, and they both hurried towards the man below them, who paused and turned at their call and now stood patiently waiting.

'I'll race you the last few yards!'

Without waiting to see if Sherry responded, Elizabeth took to her heels impulsively and ran downhill, her pale hair streaming behind her in the wind.

'Don't run!'

Dee's voice was sharp, alarmed, but his cry came too late. With an exclamation of dismay Elizabeth flung up her arms and measured her length on the soft pine needles.

Dee reached her side even quicker than he had reached Sherry at the runnel, bounding uphill as easily as if he had been running on the flat. Sherry noticed that he was not even out of the breath as he knelt beside the fallen girl and put his arms about her, lifting her gently.

'Oh, what a fool! You told us to watch our step,' groaned Elizabeth ruefully.

'Never mind that now. Lean against me for a minute.' Dee pressed her against him, and there was no sign of criticism in his face or his voice.

'If that had been me I should have caught a blasting

for being careless.' The thought flashed through Sherry's mind as she, too, bent over her friend, and she thrust it away from her as ungenerous. Dee leaned down, his vivid eyes searching.

'Let's see if you've – sprained anything.' Sherry was sure he had been about to say 'broken anything', but he checked himself after a quick glance at Elizabeth's downbent head. She raised it, and made a face.

'It's only my dignity that's damaged, not me,' she declared with a wry smile. 'The ground's too soft to cause much damage – and I'm round enough to bounce.' It was a direct slander to her slender form, but it cleared the concern from Dee's face.

'No ricks anywhere? Sure?' He caught her two hands, and made a quick inspection of her wrists.

'Positive. If you'll help me up. I'll prove it.'

'Take it steady, then.' He grasped her round the waist and rose to his own feet, drawing her up with him. She steadied herself against him while he still held her, and experimentally flexed her legs and ankles.

'No, everything works – and nothing hurts, fortunately. I should have had more sense,' she apologized. 'You told us to look out for exposed roots.' She indicated the gnarled tangle on the ground that had brought about her downfall.

'Not to worry, there's no damage done.' Dee spoke soothingly, and Sherry raised her eyebrows. Dee was certainly being easy on Elizabeth, and he didn't seem in any great hurry to release her now that she was on her feet again, she thought critically. As if he sensed what was in her mind he dropped his arm from about the girl's waist.

'You'll know not to run along the rides in future,' he smiled, and remembering the blaze of anger in his eyes when she shot the traffic lights Sherry wondered ruefully what charms her friend had that she did not possess, whatever it was it seemed to work on Dee.

'Now I've stopped you looking for our tree,' apologized the girl.

'I've already found one,' he announced in a pleased tone. 'It's right at the intersection of the two rides. Come and see it, in case it doesn't come up to your exacting standards,' he teased.

Elizabeth made a face at him, but had to admit that she could find nothing wrong with his choice when he displayed it, standing tall and proud on the edge of the aisle of trees, and on a conveniently flat piece of ground adjacent to the ride. To her secret chagrin, Sherry could not fault it either, and they both conceded game and match to their companion, to his undisguised delight as he marked the bark with a piece of chalk he had thoughtfully put in his pocket for that purpose.

'Now let's get back before the light goes.' He grasped a hand of each girl, one on either side of him, and flashed a look at the sky. Sherry felt him tense, and she looked up too in time to see a dark wedge of geese appear overhead, and tilt downwards towards the pools below them.

'They're coming in for the night,' Dee remarked matter-of-factly. 'It's time we homed, too.'

A deep tinge of pink warmed the leaden sky above them, and Sherry realized with a sense of shock that the afternoon had fled, and the sun was already setting. She hastened along beside her two companions, the strength of the man's hand over her own making it easy for her to keep up with them on the downward slope, and he did not slacken speed until he came to the path running beside the pools.

85

'We can take it easy now.'

The shingle track beside the water was rougher, with the runnels an ever-present hazard, but the light was much better here than among the trees. Looking back through them, Sherry found she could barely distinguish the separate trunks, and the whole planting above them was like a black, impenetrable curtain. It was difficult to realize that only a short half hour before it had been a multi-mixture of greens and browns, daylight-tinted, and now the daylight, at least in the plantings, was almost gone, and the silence that had seemed so peaceful to her before dropped heavily oppressive, so that Sherry was glad of the feel of Dee's hand round hers, a warm, human contact that was comforting in this suddenly alien place, even if it was the touch of someone she didn't particularly like.

Her fingers must have instinctively reflected her thoughts, for she felt Dee's tighten their grip, and he glanced down at her quickly. Perhaps he thought she was still afraid of the runnel, and she did not disabuse him, feeling faintly ashamed of her momentary nervousness, like a child unwilling to admit to being afraid of the dark. With Dee holding her she was hardly likely to slip again, particularly in the runnel confronting them, it was shallow and not very wide, so that she stepped across it easily beside him.

The water under her feet was tinted, and she looked up at the sky. She did not notice Dee's eyes linger on her upturned face, resting there thoughtfully with a quiet strength in their blue depths that was as the strength of the tall trees about them, calm and unshakeable, bending to acknowledge the force of the storms that shook them from time to time, but straightening again, tall and proud, to the high dome of the sky to which they pointed. Sherry's own eyes were turned on it still, on the strengthening colours of the sunset brilliantly reflected in the shadowy mirror of the pools that were minutely darkened here and there where the geese floated, resting with folded wings on the surface of the water that caught and held the fiery colours from the sky, as if the battle that had given the pools their name had not long faded into silence, leaving behind the redly tinted waters to gaze up in agonized protest to the unheeding sky.

She paused, and Dee spoke.

'What's the matter?'

'Nothing.' She hesitated. 'It just seems a pity to hurry away from – all this.' She waved her hand vaguely at the surrounding scenery, and Dee nodded as if he understood just what her 'all this' meant.

'You've seen it all before, dozens of times,' protested Elizabeth. 'Let's keep moving, it's cold standing still,' she shivered.

For once Sherry didn't mind the cold. And although she had seen it all before, as Elizabeth said, dozens of times, somehow this evening the beauty of it had a sharp poignancy that was almost a pain, and the keenness of it made a bitter-sweet hurt that she could not explain to herself, let alone to her companions.

CHAPTER SIX

THE phone rang just as they started breakfast the next morning. Sherry put down her porridge spoon and rose from her seat.

'I'll take it, Polly,' she called, and turned reluctant feet towards the hall. Who on earth could it be at this time in the morning? she wondered. The fact that it was a Monday, and still dark outside and bitterly cold, did nothing to help. She had slept heavily the night before, healthily tired from her outing to the conifer plantation yesterday, and still inclined to yawn her way through the breakfast that Polly insisted she swallow before she went out.

An instant of panic touched her in case her uncle had been taken ill again, but the long gossip she had had with him the evening before did not indicate anything but a one-way trip to recovery. The voice on the phone gave her immediate reassurance. It was male, cheerful, with a teasingly familiar ring, and it asked for Mr. Lawrence.

'Yours,' she told Dee with callous relief, returning to the dining-room. He gave an exclamation of disgust and rose from his seat with a reluctance to get started equal to her own. Sherry shivered, and pulled her chair closer to the fire, deserting the table in preference for the warmth of the hearth, and hugging her bowl of porridge on her knee. Polly would not approve, but she felt unaccountably depressed this morning, which was unusual for her even on a Monday. Dee seemed to be a long time on the phone. She ate her way through a piece of toast, and was reaching for a second which she wanted more as a barrier to starting the day than as food, when he reappeared through the door. He did not bother to sit down, but joined her at the fire and leaned against the mantelshelf, looking down at her.

'There's been a break-in at the garage,' he announced quietly.

'A break-in?' Sherry dropped her other piece of toast unheeded on her plate. Fully awake now, she looked up at him. 'I thought those railings had been secured?'

'It isn't into my premises, it's into yours. In Manders Motors,' he emphasized. 'That was the Panda car driver on the phone. He saw a smashed window in the workshop and went in to investigate. The lock on the gate had been forced.'

So that was why she had recognized the voice. Sherry rose abruptly and put her plate down with a clatter.

'I'll get down there right away.'

This would have to happen while her uncle was away and she was left in charge of the firm. To her knowledge they had never had a burglary of any kind before.

'I'll come with you.' Dee swallowed the last of his coffee in one gulp and made for the hall to get his coat. They had a quick word with Polly on their way out to explain the deserted breakfast-table, leaving her lamenting loudly in the kitchen about the evils of the modern world, and in a few minutes they were on their way, Dee urging their vehicle through the inhospitable darkness of early morning until they pulled up beside the now familiar striped car.

'This is becoming a habit,' thought Sherry, and felt

her throat go dry as she saw the big gates, that had always seemed so secure, swung wide, the lock dangling uselessly where it had been wrenched apart by what must have been considerable force. The Panda driver appeared out of the gloom and addressed Dee.

'Sorry to disturb you this early, Mr. Lawrence, but I thought you ought to know quickly, and maybe you could let me have some keys so that we can go through and check to see if anything's missing.'

'Sherry, you've got the keys.'

She fished a bunch out of her pocket and fitted one into the lock of the main door. It was a double one, and tricky, and it had obviously defeated the trespasser. Whoever it was had smashed one of the big windows to gain entry. And let in all the cold air straight on to the cars, thought Sherry bitterly, regretting the waste of warmth that was always kept in the building at night for the sake of easy starting-up in the mornings. Her own vehicle was pulled up fairly close to the door, and would most likely be difficult to start – the wind was blowing straight through the jagged hole.

Reaching up an accustomed hand to the light switch, she banished the shadows and gave a quick look round at the assembled vehicles. Except for the three parked near the wash yard, that Sherry knew had been used for late runs, they had all been cleaned the night before ready for the road in the morning, and the steel grey, shiny fleet was drawn up like a miniature regiment on parade, only their number plates betraying any difference between them to the uninitiated. To their drivers, each car was an individual, and Sherry knew that they each had an unofficial name. She turned a blind eye to the fact that Syd, the senior driver, called his car Polly, after an uncomfortable encounter with Humphrey Manders' housekeeper one snowy morning, when he had been half an hour late in collecting his employer. To the real Polly, time was time, and snowdrifts or not she considered he should have been there when he was expected.

'They look all right to me – oh!'

Her glance fell on several of the cars, her own included, grouped in a corner of the garage near to the door. The doors had all been wrenched open and the boot lids were up. She checked the contents quickly. A scatter of tow-ropes, jacks and shovels had been flung on to the garage floor, as if they were of no interest to whoever searched the cars. Sherry made to slam the nearest boot lid shut, and the policeman checked her quickly.

'I should leave it where it is, miss,' he said, in a tone that brooked no argument, and Sherry desisted hastily. This was not the friendly policeman she knew, but the voice of authority. 'Perhaps you'll examine the rest of your fleet, and then go over the office quarters to see if there's any sign of interference anywhere else? Maybe Mr. Lawrence will go with you,' as Dee approached. He had been having a prowl round the garage on his own account, a fact that Sherry did not know whether to feel relieved or vexed about. The premises were not his to prowl in, without her permission, and yet if there was an intruder still lurking in them ... She shivered.

'I'll come with you.'

Dee's voice was a statement, not a question, and he circled the garage with her, looking minutely into each of the other cars, checking their boots and lockers, and Sherry followed him checking too, reluctantly glad of his company in the eerie, early-morning silence of the big building.

When they reached the workshop office, they found it in a state of chaos. The desk drawers had all been tossed on to the floor, and an accumulation of pens, note pads and paper clips littered the mat.

'If whoever it was thought they would have found any money in here, they should have known better,' snapped Sherry. 'We never keep much petty cash, thank goodness, and that's always locked in the safe in the main office. Heavens! I wonder if . . .' She did not stop to finish her sentence, but headed for the main office across the yard with hurried steps. To her relief she found the door still locked, and she fumbled with the key and opened it hastily.

'This office is too close to the road to be attractive to a burglar,' said Dee, flicking on the light. The fluorescent glow proved the truth of his words, the safe and everything in the room was untouched, just as they had left it the night before. Nevertheless they stopped to make a thorough check before rejoining the policeman and giving him a report on their search.

'Come inside the office and I'll make a cup of coffee,' offered Sherry, regarding his frozen visage. 'It's bitterly cold here with the doors wide open.'

She expected him to accept with the same alacrity that he had shown before, and regarded him with astonishment when he remained woodenly where he was.

'Thanks, but I'll stay here with the cars, if you don't mind.'

His tone suggested that he didn't care whether she minded or not.

'I've rung up the station, and they're sending the Inspector over right away,' he informed her.

'Why?' asked Sherry, wondering at his need of reinforcements. 'Nothing seems to have been stolen, and the cars haven't been damaged in any way. 'It's probably only some youths on a pre-Christmas spree,' she hazarded, and trailed into silence at the unforthcoming look on the policeman's face.

'Why not make that coffee anyhow?' suggested Dee tactfully. 'We could do with a cup ourselves, and maybe the officer will have one when he's finished here.'

'A good idea, sir.' Even his voice was unsmiling, Sherry thought. 'And while you're about it, miss, perhaps you would make a list of the runs your cars have done over the past week or ten days. Maybe one of your drivers has picked up a passenger who got the idea of breaking in here in case you kept the fare money on the premises,'

'But we never do,' replied Sherry in a bewildered tone of voice. 'It's always put in the night safe at the bank round the corner. By the time all the cars have come in and checked in their takings for the day it usually amounts to quite a big sum, though of course a lot of our regulars pay by cheque. Still, I'll list the runs for you, and when the drivers clock in they'll be able to help with descriptions and so on,' she added helpfully.

'If you could start on the lists for me now, miss,' the officer hinted, and Sherry turned away towards the office, with Dee beside her. 'You'll stay on the premises, won't you?' the policeman called after her. 'The Inspector might want to ask you a few questions, and you'll be able to provide the answers easier than anyone else.' He unbent a little at Sherry's startled look.

'He seems to be making a lot of fuss, it isn't as if there's been anything taken, as far as I can see, and the cars haven't been ill-used,' grumbled Sherry, shrugging out of her coat in the warm office. Nevertheless, the familar feel of her surroundings was comforting; it was disturbing to think that anyone could get on to the premises at night, and there was also the problem of telling her uncle. She did not want him to come back all the way from Devon, and perhaps undo all the good his holiday was doing him. She sighed, her gaze on the slowly lightening square of the window. They say trouble never comes on its own, she thought ruefully, and since her uncle's departure trouble had arrived with a vengeance, and looked as if it was drawing more unwelcome companions in its wake. She saw Ben's portly figure appear through the gate; he was always earlier than anyone else in arriving at work because it was his job to unlock the premises in the morning. The expression on his face was comically concerned at finding his task already done, and a police car confronting him from just inside the yard. His eyes flew to the lighted office window, and he homed towards it with hurried steps.

'Come in, Ben,' Sherry called. 'Have a coffee,' she invited.

'Whatever's the matter, miss? What are the police doing here? There's nothing wrong with Mr. Manders, is there?' he questioned, all in one breath.

'No, thank goodness!' Sherry felt that she could count her blessings on that one score, at least. 'There's been a break-in, but there's no damage done, nor anything taken, so far as we can tell,' she forestalled the elderly mechanic's questions. 'All that's happened as far as I can see is that a few of the cars have been searched, and the workshop office tipped upside down.' She turned a troubled face to him. 'When you've finished your coffee, Ben, go over the garage as well, will you?' she begged. 'Mr. Lawrence and I have checked it over, but you're more likely to spot anything amiss than we are. We've already checked all the car boots, but there doesn't seem to be anything missing.'

'I'll get along and have a look now, miss.'

Ben finished his drink with a quick swallow, and clattered the empty cup down on her desk. He could drink scalding coffee quicker than anyone Sherry knew. His daily ration of doughy cake must act like an asbestos lining on his tummy, she thought wonderingly.

'You were going to get the police a list of runs,' reminded Dee.

'List of ... oh, that. I can soon get that from the car logs,' Sherry sat down on her swivel chair and reached into the pigeon hole of records at the side of her desk. Her own car log came out on top. 'Let's see, two runs to the airport, one mum-to-be to the maternity hospital, two theatregoers and six runs to the station, and a woman with more money than sense on a shopping expedition. She took all morning, and the hire of the car cost her enough to buy a dress,' she marvelled. 'Apart from the regulars that we get every week, that accounts for about the lot on my own car. It's been fairly quiet, except for the weddings at the week-end.' Meticulously she added those to her list, which despite what she said still added up to a formidable amount of work when taken in conjunction with running the administrative side of the business. 'Now for the others,' she drew the pile of logs to her.

Dee looked over her shoulder at what she had already written.

'If that's just a list of your own runs, I'd have thought you could do with more time in the office while your uncle's away,' he remarked casually.

Sherry flushed. The fury she had felt when they first got to the garage that morning returned now in full force, and stopped her flood of words stillborn. She picked up her desk rule and gripped it until her knuckles showed white. Desperately she concentrated on the markings. They were the old-fashioned ones, it should be metric now. She would have to buy a new one the next time she was in town with a minute to spare. The mundane thought steadied her, and her throat unlocked itself.

'I'm quite capable of deciding that for myself,' she began, her words coming taut through the jaws that ached with clenching. It took all her self-control to speak quietly; she felt like shouting at Dee to go away and look after his own firm, and leave her to look after Manders Motors on her own. Why, oh, why had the storm happened this winter? Of all the winters gone by, when her uncle was safely in control, why could it not have happened then and saved her the necessity of having to take into the office the one person she most desired to keep firmly off the premises.

'This is Miss Manders, Inspector.'

The door opened and admitted 'their' policeman, as Sherry called him to herself, though she had doubts now about wishing to claim ownership, the friendly young policeman was one thing, and this suddenly remote, professional guardian of the law quite another.

'Sorry to trouble you, Miss Manders, but it'll be

better for everyone if we can get a few things cleared up quickly, then we can leave you to get on.' The Inspector seemed friendly enough. 'I'm Wallace, C.I.D., by the way.' He held out an identity card, his eyes meeting hers with a friendly light in them that belied his crisp tone. She smiled back at him, relaxing for the first time since she had reached the premises that morning. The C.I.D. man was short, not much more than her own height, and about as slender, and all her previous conceptions about C.I.D. Inspectors – entirely gained from the television, she admitted – vanished in a rush. This man was human. She responded immediately, her hand moving to the still full coffee pot with a questioning glance in his direction.

'I'd love one, and I expect my officer would too. He's been standing in the wind too long to feel very warm,' he guessed.

Sherry filled two cups, feeling a sense of unreality about the whole business. She handed one to the Inspector and the other to the policeman, who promptly got his smile back. Sherry pushed her lists over the desk towards the man opposite her.

'This is the lot for the last week. I don't know how it can help, there seems to be no damage done, and nothing taken,' she offered.

'We want to find the people responsible,' he responded briskly. 'There are too many of these petty break-ins at this time of the year. Christmas, you know,' he said, and smiled at Sherry's shocked look. 'It doesn't mean the same thing to everyone, Miss Manders,' he added sadly. 'To a lot of the do-badders it means the opportunity for easy money. You'd be surprised at the number of these calls we get round about this season,' he said, his voice abdicating his faith in human nature.

'There doesn't seem to be any money missing,' Sherry pointed out, and he shook his head.

'That's probably because whoever broke in was disturbed. Maybe they saw the Panda car, or heard the officer coming to take a look. Whatever disturbed your burglar you were lucky they didn't take their disappointment out on your vehicles,' he commented. 'There's a good deal of vandalism about nowadays, and half an hour of so-called "fun" on the part of a delinquent can do a good many pounds' worth of damage,' he told her on a note of bitter experience. 'You've got a valuable fleet of cars in there,' he pointed out unnecessarily.

It was a fact of which Sherry was keenly aware, and it made her feel the weight of her responsibility even more heavily. If only the break-in hadn't happened! It was bad enough having the storm – and having to shelter its 'orphan' – she thought, without anything else happening while she was in charge. She had so desperately wanted everything to go well while she held the reins, and now this had to happen. If only her uncle was back! She shook herself angrily. It was no use wishing, she had to face what had happened whether she liked it or not, and she found that she liked it less with each passing day. Her uncle had been right, it was no job for a woman, and she would be heartily thankful when things were back to normal again and she could hand over her responsibilities to shoulders more fitted to bear them. The Inspector had said she was lucky. It was luck that she could well do without, she reflected bitterly, and sent up a fervent hope that there was no more of its kind on the way.

The C.I.D. man ran an interested eye down her list,

and then stuffed it carefully into his wallet.

'I hear the airport had to close the flying field on the day of the storm,' he remarked conversationally. 'Was it long before it got going again?'

'They were in operation the next day,' returned Sherry, surprised that he seemed to be unaware of the fact. Perhaps the police didn't know everything, after all. Another of her misconceptions released its hold on life, and she sighed. It was a bit like finding out the truth about Father Christmas. It made one feel suddenly old.

'When I got there in the morning they had been accepting incoming flights for some time, and the outgoings were running almost normally. That was about mid-morning or just after,' she remembered, timing it by the fact that she and Dee had been eating their ginger cake when the call came.

'I shouldn't imagine they would get many passengers at this time of year.' The Inspector seemed settled for a friendly gossip, and under the warmth of his approach Sherry relaxed. Her normally cheerful nature was tired of the antagonism that she could not help but feel towards Dee, and she responded readily to the casual ease of the man confronting her.

'Not a lot,' she replied, 'though the lounge was full enough the day before.'

'Christmas holidaymakers, I suppose,' said the Inspector, and in his voice she detected a note of envy.

'I expect so.' Sherry sighed, sharing his feelings. It would be lovely to fly to faraway places, out of reach of the winter cold for a spell, she thought wistfully. Suddenly she felt tired of freezing days and bitter nights, and storms that wrecked other people's buildings and poured their problems – and them – on to her own unwilling head. It would be nice to just drop everything for a couple of weeks or so, and fly away and forget about it all.

She looked up at the Inspector to tell him so, and found the eyes of the three men watching her, each with a different expression in them.

Those of the Panda car driver were professionally impersonal, the way he had looked at her when he had refused her offer of coffee earlier. The Inspector's gaze was clear and bright, rapier-keen, as if he looked right through her to the wall and back, thought Sherry, startled, and had an uneasy feeling that she did not need to tell him what she was thinking, he could already read her thoughts for himself as easily as if she had spoken them out loud.

The other pair of eyes of a clear, periwinkle blue, held a clouded look that could have been either concern or disapproval. It was probably the latter, thought Sherry resignedly. Dee seemed to automatically disapprove of most things she did. It could not be concern, she decided. She meant as little to him as he did to her. For the second time that morning, depression descended on her like one of the dark clouds glooming overhead, revealed by the strengthening daylight to be filling a sky that by its colour threatened early snow.

CHAPTER SEVEN

THE snow held off, and it got warmer as the day progressed, bringing with it a thin drizzle that froze into a sheet of ice on the roads when the temperature dropped again with vindictive rapidity in the small hours of the next morning.

Dee tried his brakes cautiously as he eased the van out of the gates of Arne Cottage on their way to work.

'Hold tight, we're sliding!'

He had no need to warn her. Sherry had felt the tyres loose their grip and was already hanging on to the grab rail on the door beside her.

'Black ice!'

The back wheels confirmed every driver's dread by performing a half circle under them, and Dee nursed the van carefully until it found its grip again on the treacherous surface. He had made a habit of taking her to work every morning since he had stayed at Arne Cottage. It saved her the trouble of bringing out her own Mini, and she was always reluctant to make use of a fleet car for private purposes. Besides their being expensive on petrol, and a nuisance to park because of sheer size, she knew that Ben liked his flock in at night for their evening wash and brush-up, and it had become a habit for her and Dee to travel together. At first she had hesitated, with the reluctance of every driver to accept the role of passenger in another person's vehicle, but her instinctive nervousness quickly subsided, and she travelled beside Dee now as happily as if she had been at the wheel herself.

He pulled up at the gates of Manders Motors to let her get out, then took the van on into his own premises opposite. Sherry paused in the act of unlocking the office door, and looked across the road towards Beacon Hire. The whole of the second storey looked like a gigantic Christmas package, she thought, wrapped in the silver-coloured plastic sheeting. She swung the door open and kicked against a pile of post on the mat. Unenthusiastically she bent to pick it up. She did not feel much like coping with paperwork this morning. Rationally or otherwise, she felt constantly on her guard when she was with Dee, and the strain of it was beginning to make her feel irritable. It was not as if she had any break away from it when she got home, because he was there in the house with her as well, so that it was impossible to avoid his company without causing comment.

'I'd love a trip across the downs this morning,' she thought. Maybe the airport would ring and want some baggage collected, or a passenger. They did most days, even in the winter. In spite of the road conditions, she felt a sudden urgency for solitude, a need to get away from people and problems for a while, and perhaps most of all the need to get away from a sudden restlessness within her own self that seemed to grow stronger with every passing, unsatisfactory day.

'If Mr. Manders rings, don't mention the fact that we've had a break-in, will you?' she asked Ben later. 'I don't want him worried.' She had said nothing to him on the telephone when she made her usual call the night before, thinking it best to let the matter drop unless anything came of the police inquiries, when of course he would have to know, but he would be stronger by then, maybe even back at home. 'It might be as well to warn the others, in case one of them answers the switchboard if you happen to be out for any reason,' she went on. It was a small board, and either Ben, or Paul the apprentice coped with the incoming calls, radioing messages out to the nearest available car. A large-scale map of the district with coloured flags – Paul's proud invention – hung on the wall beside the board, and showed the current destination of each car, making it a simple matter to see which one was the nearest to a fresh call at any given time.

'I'm off now to take that couple to the station for the early train to London,' she told the mechanic. 'Someone else going on holiday,' she thought wistfully, and hoped the day would bring in something interesting in the way of a run for her. It had been a quiet morning so far as she was concerned, and she felt too restless to want to remain cooped in the office. 'Better to be cooped in a moving car,' she thought wryly. The storm, and having Dee, and now the break-in, had shaken her usually cheerful resilience, and this morning she felt that she just could not bounce back.

The sight of Elizabeth on the station platform, bidding good-bye to some visitors about to board the same train as her own passengers, seemed like one bright spot in the surrounding gloom, and Sherry hailed her thankfully.

'Come and have a coffee,' Elizabeth called back in response to her wave. 'I'm free now our visitors have gone,' she explained, joining her, 'and you look down in the dumps,' she added, eyeing Sherry closely.

'We've had a break-in at the garage.'

Thankful to find a sympathetic ear, Shery poured

out her story of the happenings of the day before, and Elizabeth took it all with deflating calm.

'I know,' she said, reaching for the sugar. 'Dee told me yesterday. We met up when he was making a delivery to the works,' she explained, 'and gave me the news then. Are you going to tell your uncle about it?' she inquired, unashamedly licking jam from her fingers where her over-generous hand had made it ooze from the middle of her scone.

'No!' Sherry's voice was forceful. 'He mustn't know, it would only worry him, and its senseless to do that now. It isn't as if there's been anything stolen, or much damage done except a broken window.' A thought struck her. 'Dee mustn't tell him, either.' The fact that he had mentioned it to Elizabeth was disconcerting.

'I don't think he would, without asking you,' soothed her friend, giving a keen glance at Sherry's disturbed face. 'He only mentioned it to me in passing – among a lot of other things,' she smiled.

'What sort of things, I wonder?' The thought flashed through Sherry's mind, and she shook it away, but it returned to pester her. Dee hadn't mentioned that he had seen Elizabeth yesterday, although they'd spent the evening together in the drawing-room at Arne Cottage, one on each side of the fire. Like Darby and Joan, thought Sherry disgustedly, and about as talkative, she turning the pages of a magazine, too restless to concentrate on the printed words, and Dee quietly sketching. Her mind was too occupied with the break-in even to be interested in what he was drawing. When Polly brought in the bedtime drink and biscuits at half-past nine, Sherry took it from her hands thankfully, glad of a diversion for the silence was becoming painful, and Dee quietly closed his pad and joined her at the tray as if he, too, was relieved that the evening was nearly over.

He might have told me he'd seen Elizabeth, thought Sherry resentfully; she's my friend, not Dee's. Wasn't she? Despite herself, Sherry could not erase from her mind the picture of Dee helping up Elizabeth after her tumble on the way down from the plantation. She had thought then that he had seemed in no hurry to remove his arm from about her waist, and the girl had not made any objection. But Elizabeth was in love with Andy – wasn't she? Suddenly, Sherry felt unsure about a lot of things that had seemed so comfortably stable before. That Andy was more than fond of Elizabeth was evident enough to anyone who cared to read the frank, open face of the young Canadian businessman, and until now Sherry had felt sure that Elizabeth reciprocated his feelings, but people could change their minds, persisted her thoughts. After all, it was said to be a woman's privilege. What if Elizabeth had decided to exercise it?

This is nonsense, she thought, stopping the questions angrily. Dee had only met Elizabeth a few times. As far as you know, the voice inside her persisted. Its prodding drove her to her feet in hasty movement. She swallowed the rest of her coffee at a gulp and looked at her watch.

'Half-past twelve? It can't be!' She stared at the hands, horrified. 'I'd no idea we'd sat here for so long.' Elizabeth's enthusiastic recounting of plans for the forthcoming children's party, and her hopes of actually seeing the tree felled and brought down from the plantation, had been more time-consuming than she had realized.

'You must come and watch it cut down too. You

never know, we might even be able to help,' her friend suggested.

Her enthusiasm seemed to be more centred on the tree than on the party itself, thought Sherry observantly, and wondered if the fact that Dee was providing the transport for it had anything to do with her friend's preoccupation with this part of the arrangements. Just the same she would like to see the Christmas tree felled, she thought, it would be an interesting experience to watch it actually taken down, though she had her doubts about the helping bit. Mainly, that if she herself offered to help Dee would undoubtedly refuse, and if she tried to give a hand anyway what she did would probably be wrong, whatever she did usually seemed to be, in Dee's eyes, though he appeared to approve of Elizabeth.

'I'll have to fly.' She got up from her seat abruptly. 'Ben will wonder where on earth I am. I usually ring him and let him know if I'm going anywhere apart from the scheduled trip,' she explained her haste. 'I'm over an hour adrift, and he fusses a bit.' She felt slightly ashamed of her lack of consideration for Ben, but she would soon be back in the garage and able to reassure him. 'I needed a gossip to somebody,' she confided.

Elizabeth regarded her thoughtfully.

'Why not take a day off, and go shopping? You must have some to do, this near to Christmas,' she pointed out. 'It would do you good to have a break away from the garage. It's been all work for you just lately.'

'And storm and burglary,' added Sherry ruefully. 'I was just getting grumpy, that's all,' she admitted, 'but I might take your advice about the shopping, I hate a last-minute rush and this year I shall be landed with one,' she realized. She had already got her uncle's and aunt's presents, they had gone with the car to Devon, with an extracted promise from their future owners not to open until Christmas, but there was still Polly's, and one for Elizabeth, and then there was Ben and . . . 'I'll take the afternoon off,' she decided, and immediately felt better. At this time of year, and at Easter, both times popular for weddings and in consequence busy for the cars, she usually had to have her time-off during the week, and she had not had any days to speak of since her uncle was first taken ill.

The early ice had melted under a thin sun, and she made better speed on the road back to the garage than she had dared to do on the outward journey. She swung in at the gates, parked her car on the wash yard ready for Paul, and ran lightly up the office steps humming a snatch of the latest hit tune on the radio. Ben turned a worried face towards her as she stepped inside the door, and Dee rose swiftly from the wooden chair that he still retained for his use rather than use Humphrey Manders' more comfortable swivel one.

'Where in heaven's name have you been?'

His eyes, furiously angry, bored into hers as they had done on the day she shot the traffic lights.

'I was getting bothered about you, Miss Sherry,' began Ben, and she turned to him contritely.

'I'm sorry, Ben, I should have rung you. I know I usually do, but I met Elizabeth Lomax and . . .'

'And started gossiping, I suppose, without a scrap of consideration for people who might be concerned for your safety,' gritted Dee, and Sherry spun round on him, stung into anger.

'I forgot to ring the garage – is that a crime? And in any case, whether I ring in or not is no concern of yours,' she flashed. 'My uncle asked you to keep an eye on the business,' she reminded him angrily, 'but you're not in charge, of either it or me. Do I have to remind you of that on a daily basis?' she cried.

'We were worried, like I said, Miss Sherry.' The normally quiet Ben intervened. 'Mr. Lawrence, as well as me,' he pointed out, and something in his tone stemmed the angry flow of words on Sherry's tongue. 'There's been a big pile-up on the main road where it approaches the town by the West Gate. One of them multiple things,' he enlarged expressively. 'There was a lot of black ice on the surface . . .'

'And now there are a lot of patients in the local hospital, and three in the mortuary. One of them a woman, and unidentified. Now do you realize why Ben was worried?' Dee stressed the 'Ben', as if he personally couldn't have cared less, and Sherry went white.

'Well, you won't have to worry about me this afternoon,' she snapped, and turned to Ben, deliberately presenting her back to Dee. 'I thought of taking it off and going shopping, if there's nothing much coming in in the way of calls?'

'There's been hardly anything all morning,' said Ben, 'and it's time you took an hour or two off. You haven't had any since the boss was took bad. The drivers can cope with whatever comes in. They've had their time-off regular all the way through.'

'I could fit in a trip to the airport.' Sherry felt guilty, taking the afternoon at short notice. She did not see the hard look that Dee threw in Ben's direction, and neither, apparently, did Ben.

'Mr. Lawrence said Syd or one of the other drivers was to take all the airport calls for a week or two, Miss Sherry.' Ben looked at her doubtfully.

'Mr. Lawrence said – what?'

The office seemed to rock about Sherry. A sense of unreality possessed her, and she stared at Ben as if she did not believe the evidence of her own ears.

'There was good reason, miss,' Ben looked thoroughly unhappy.

'There is no reason, no reason at all – that gives you the right to instruct my staff.' She spoke to Dee, her voice dangerously quiet. With a supreme effort of self-control she kept her tone low, betraying nothing of the violent trembling that had started inside her from an anger such as she had never known before. It gave her face a pinched, drawn look that moved Ben to speech.

'Are you all right, miss?'

'I'm perfectly all right.' She was not. Her heart pounded with slow, agonized thuds, and her throat felt so stiff she had difficulty in enunciating. The scene had taken on a nightmarish quality of the kind when you want to scream and run, and find yourself rooted to the spot, she thought desperately. She swallowed, and tried again.

'There are only two people who have the right to give instructions at Manders Motors.' Now she had got started, the words flowed more easily. 'One is my uncle, and in his absence I am the other. Unless he has said otherwise. Has he?' she asked Dee, her attitude of polite inquiry as she waited for his answer. 'Well?' when he hesitated.

'No – but . . .'

'There are no buts,' she said shortly, and turned back to Ben. 'The trips will be taken in rotation as they always have been. If I want any alteration I'll tell you. While I'm out this afternoon Syd will take my calls as he always has done, and when I return to-morrow we'll run as usual.' She felt in her pocket for the office key, and held it out to Ben. 'Will you lock up at closing time, please, and keep the key on you until the morning. You can return it to me then.' She felt if Ben gave it to Dee afterwards she really would scream. Even now, she felt her self-control slipping, and a choking feeling akin to tears in her throat. She must not lose face in front of Dee. With a swift glance at her desk to see that everything was clear as she had left it when she went out, she turned to the door, holding it open for Ben to follow her 'I'll take my own Mini,' she told him quietly, in a tone that stopped further comment from him, and turned towards the shed where it was parked before Ben should see the trembling that threatened to take possession of her body, and make her legs reluctant to carry her.

The small car was like a toy in her hands after the big grey vehicle she had just brought in, and she spun it easily across the yard, conscious of Dee appearing at the office door, hearing but ignoring his shout of 'Sherry!' and then she was away, and parking the Mini in the market square, heading for the bank and then the shops in the hurly-burly of the Christmas shopping crowds, thankful for once of the press of people about her, seasonally cheerful in the crush, and blessedly able to hide, mostly from herself, the painful confusion in her mind as she forced it to concentrate on her purchases, and the odd ache inside her that seemed to have nothing to concentrate on, and consequently would not go away.

Despite her upset, hunger defeated her at last. She had not stopped for lunch, had partaken nothing since breakfast but the scone and coffee she had had with Elizabeth at mid-morning, and a growing void inside her made her at last glance at her watch. Subconsciously she had been aware for some time that the crowds had thinned, and it was with no surprise that she found the hands pointing to after five o'clock. Curling her arms carefully round her precious purchases, she headed back to the market square and her Mini. Even the street traders there were packing up, doubtless thinking of home and a warm fire after standing in the icy wind all day plying their wares. One man was packing what was left of his stock of Christmas trees into the back of a van. He moved over to make room for Sherry to pass, and smiled at her armful of parcels.

'Top them up with a Christmas tree, luv,' he suggested cheerfully. 'Look, I've still got this one left out. It's a shame to put it back in the van,' he wheedled, sensing a customer. Sherry paused, hesitating. Her arms were full, but the Mini wasn't far away. The man saw her glance at the nearby car park. 'I'll carry it over for you, dearie,' he offered, determined not to let her go. Sherry looked at the tree. It was a nice one, nearly three feet high, a miniature of the tall spruces they had walked among on Sunday. 'Here, you can have a log to stand it in as well,' the trader offered, and she capitulated. Christmas wouldn't seem Christmas without a tree. It looked like being a bleak one without Uncle Humph anyway, and a tree might help. She could decorate it tonight. Anything rather than spend another evening flicking over the pages of a magazine, with silence like a tangible cloud between her and Dee.

'I'll take it,' she nodded, 'If you'll carry it over to my car for me.'

The man hastily complied, bringing the log with him as well, and he carefully stowed it in the front seat alongside her.

'It's a pity to crush it in the boot, it might damage the branches,' he said, leaning it gently against the upholstery.

'It's lovely,' She ran her eyes over the soft young fronds, and her glance met the trader's, two people unexpectedly in accord over the beauty of a young fir tree. She thought of him when they had finished dinner that evening, and she had found out the decorations ready to dress the branches. The hole in the log was a bit too big for the circumference of the small trunk, but it would do for now, she would pack it tighter when she had finished. One by one she tied the bright baubles on the tree, the gay colours and glistening silver bells vivid in the soft lamplight of the room. She felt her throat constrict, and sudden tears misted her eyes. She and Uncle Humph always did this together. A wave of desolation took her, and she wished she had not started on the tree tonight. Tomorrow would have done just as well. She might be feeling less miserable then. Dinner had been a silent meal, Dee drawing into himself with the reserve that she had been accustomed to from him before the storm, and Sherry herself felt too miserable to want speech, or indeed food tonight. Despite her earlier hunger she found she did not want Polly's excellent meal when it was put before her, and risked a scolding from the houskeeper by leaving half of it on her plate. The tree slipped sideways in the too-large hole, and she grasped it hastily to prevent it from falling over. If only Uncle Humph was back ... A firm hand caught the tree, and she jumped. She had not heard Dee cross the carpet, did not know how long he had been standing behind her.

'Let me fix it for you.' His voice was quiet, and he looked straight into her face before she had time to turn away, his eyes taking in the traces of tears on her cheeks, so that his remoteness melted, and his voice softened. 'A bit of packing here will do it nicely. Will you hold it where you want it, while I stuff the hole?'

Automatically she reached out and steadied the tree, as she would have done for her uncle, and he smiled a brief thank-you, a smile that took some of the ache away from inside her, she did not know why. He busied himself for a few minutes, then straightened up and she tried the tree experimentally, but Dee had packed the hole firmly, and it held stable. Suddenly she felt she wanted to finish decorating it, and she shook out the remaining balls and tinsel strings from the box with an enthusiasm she had not felt all the evening. In silence, Dee reached out a hand to hold the branches while she tied, tying the higher ones for her when she had to stand on tiptoe to reach, but it was a companionable, easy silence, not the pulling-down of shutters between them as it had been over dinner.

Finished at last, they stepped back to survey their handiwork, pleased as children with the brightly dressed tree which even brought a smile to Polly's face as she came in with the supper tray.

'Goodness, I'd no idea it was that time!' exclaimed Sherry, wondering where the evening had flown to as she took her cup and a biscuit to her uncle's chair beside the fire, picking up the evening paper on the way as a cover for her lap. Automatically, she turned the news sheet the right way up, and black headlines glared at her over an almost full-page photograph.

'That's the pile-up by the West Gate this morning.' Dee sat down opposite to her, his eyes resting on her face.

Sherry caught her breath. The photographer had

taken a close-up of a tangled heap of vehicles of all kinds, some of them so closely intertwined in a mass of twisted metal as to be indistinguishable one from the other. She caught her breath sharply, and looked up with horrified eyes to her companion.

'I knew the ice on the road was bad this morning, but this . . .' Her eyes were drawn downwards with dreadful fascination to the pictured destruction on her knee.

'It was very bad across the downs, on the road to the airport,' responded Dee seriously. 'Inside the town walls it was treacherous enough, but out there across the hills . . .' He broke off, shaking his head.

'Did you have a trip across yourself, then?'

'Yes,' he responded briefly, 'and I found it difficult enough to hold my own van on the road, and my arms are a lot stronger than yours,' he added significantly.

'I can hold my car, even if it's a big one,' Sherry spoke up defensively against his implied criticism of her abilities as a driver. He had criticized her once before, and he had been wrong then. He had acknowledged it, too, her sense of fairness told her, and she stifled it unrepentantly. She had driven through enough winters without mishap. But not across the road to the downs in the worst of the winter, her thoughts persisted, and she shrugged them away irritably. She didn't do a lot of driving during midwinter anyway; her uncle always wanted her in the office with him, for the stocktaking, which took several weeks to get through because Humphrey Manders usually wanted his lists checked and re-checked, and Sherry humoured him, knowing him to be a stickler for exactitude in even the smallest detail. But it could have been a ploy on his part, she realized now, to keep her in the garage during the icy weather, and still spare her feelings. She had never suspected him before, but once the doubt had entered her mind it grew and took hold, making her perversely even more determined to go her own way without interference on Dee's part.

'I can hold my own vehicle,' she repeated stubbornly, aware that Dee was watching her gravely.

'That's what the woman in the crash probably thought,' he responded soberly. 'According to the paper, they still haven't identified her.'

'My uncle never tried to stop me from driving the big cars in icy weather,' Sherry answered him defiantly, stifling the doubts she had that her uncle might have used a kinder but equally effective method of restricting her driving activities during the periods when the state of the roads was an additional menace to the already hazardous occupation she had chosen to share with his staff. She had had one or two narrow escapes – what professional driver hadn't? But her own skill, of which she was justly proud, had given her a quiet confidence in her own ability that she knew to be fully justified, and Dee's efforts at restraining her now had touched where it hurt.

'Maybe your uncle hasn't forbidden you before. That's his privilege while he's in charge of you, but now ...'

'You're not in charge of me!' Sherry stopped him short, her eyes flashing, a small, defiant figure stiff with indignation, and a momentary gleam appeared in the man's eyes.

'If you'll calm down,' he snapped, 'I was only going to suggest that your uncle has got enough to worry about with his own health at the moment, without having a possible crashed car as well, with you inside it,' he finished, deliberately brutal. 'No driver on earth can control a car when it takes off over black ice – which is what happened at the West Gate today,' he went on remorselessly, 'and I for one don't want the job of telling him that you've been hauled off to hospital and your car to the breaker's yard – or worse,' he finished significantly.

'I hadn't thought of that.' Suddenly sobered, Sherry thought of the effect of such news on her uncle, and immediately shut her mind to its possibilities. 'It might give him . . .'

'It can't, if it doesn't happen,' responded Dee more gently now, 'But you do see why?'

'Yes, I'm sorry.' She wasn't really, but it would be indecent not to apologise for her angry words.

'Then forget it now.' Dee removed the paper from under her eyes that were brooding on the picture on the front page. 'Eat your supper and let's talk about something else for a while, or you'll be dreaming about it. But for the sake of my peace of mind, promise you won't take your car over the road across the downs while this weather lasts,' he demanded firmly.

CHAPTER EIGHT

'You're not still worrying about the crash, are you?'

Dee glanced across the office to where Sherry sat at her own desk, abstractedly biting the end of her pencil, and frowning into the distance.

'Mmm?' His comment registered, and she clicked the pencil back into its glass tray. 'I wasn't worrying – at least, not about that,' she said frankly.

'Then what?'

'I was thinking about Polly's Christmas present. I've got her some woolly vests,' she answered his query, 'and somehow they don't seem very interesting as a present. I thought I might tuck a pretty box of talc or something in with them, if I can get to the shops before they close.'

'I didn't know they sold black vests,' remarked Dee wickedly.

'They don't, they're white wool and nylon – oh!' Realization that they were discussing Polly's more intimate wearing apparel turned her cheeks scarlet, and she glowered at him.

'There's a call from the airport, miss.'

Ben's head appeared through the door and he regarded Sherry dubiously. He had given her the office key as she had instructed, when they came in first thing, but he was obviously unhappy about the relationship between her and Dee, and his face reflected his feelings.

'Come in Ben, it's all right,' Sherry assured him. 'Is Syd in? Then send him,' as the mechanic nodded, and was immediately glad of her decision when Ben's face cleared and his normal sunny look reaffixed itself. 'I'll take the town trips only until the weather clears, if it's going to save you any worry,' she promised, realizing with a guilty pang that she hadn't really been fair to Ben either.

The mechanic smiled in a relieved fashion.

'Shall I leave the door open, miss?' he asked as he made to go out again. 'You look a bit warm,' he commented, his eyes on Sherry's flushed cheeks.

'No need, Ben, we're going out,' Dee replied for her. 'I'm giving Miss Manders a lift into town,' he went on. 'She wants something to go with some woolly vests,' he enlarged shyly.

Sherry could have slapped him.

Conscious of her burning face, she fled for his van which was mercifully pulled up just outside the office door, and did not dare trust her voice until he drew into the car park in the market square about twenty minutes later.

'There's Liz!' she exclaimed, seeing her friend in the act of getting out of her car further along the park. 'Cooee!' she opened the door quickly, intent on attracting her attention.

'Half a minute!' Dee grabbed the back of her jacket in time to stop her from slipping off the edge of the seat. 'remember you're in the van, not the car,' he cried.

Sherry had forgotten, and he had saved her from an undignified descent on to hard tarmac from the high vehicle, though his obvious amusement did not add to her gratitude.

'I wish he'd stop treating me like a two-year-old,' she thought irritably, all the old vexation returning in a rush. She wriggled free from his grasp, checked her

118

descent to a more modest speed, and succeeded in attracting Elizabeth's attention.

'You can come with me now you're here,' her friend announced. 'I'm off to get some more decorations for the children's Christmas tree. Those we saved from last year are looking a bit the worse for wear, and I want the fairy on the top to look her best,' she said. 'How long have you got to spare?' she asked them both impartially.

Sherry looked at Dee uncertainly. He had run her in, but he might be in a hurry himself.

'I've only got to get some talc and perhaps a few other odds and ends,' she qualified, sending a scowl in Dee's direction in case he should repeat his comments about the vests. He returned her look blandly, and made an even worse bloomer.

'She's got all the time in the world,' he announced. 'She won't be doing any airport runs until the weather clears, so there's no need to hurry back to the garage.'

He spoke as if he employed her, thought Sherry furiously, giving her glare more venom. His whole attitude rankled, and did nothing to improve her humour.

'I'm going shopping myself,' Dee informed the girls, who both looked surprised. 'I do have friends too,' he said dryly, 'so I've got a bit of Christmas shopping to do as well. If you like to be at the Royal about eleven o'clock,' he went on expansively, 'I'll treat you to a coffee.'

With a quick nod in their direction he strode off and left them to attend to their own shopping, and they only saw him once during the morning, in the High Street, just as he was about to enter a shop.

'He must have a very special friend,' remarked Elizabeth. It was a jeweller's shop Dee was going into, the best in Beacon Downs, and Sherry watched his tall figure with interest as he ducked under the lintel and disappeared into the carpeted dimness of the interior.

'What are you going to get him for Christmas?' asked her companion curiously.

'Get Dee a Christmas present?' Sherry regarded Elizabeth with dismay. 'I hadn't thought . . .'

She hadn't thought, but she realized with a sinking heart that she would have to, and quickly. Christmas was already within touching distance, and as Dee would be staying at Arne cottage with them she could not give a present to Polly and not have one to give to Dee. Suppose he gave her one? That possibility hadn't occurred to her, either, and the thought made her hot with embarrassment.

'I'd thought of getting him a set of cuff-links. After all, he's giving me a lot of help with the tree,' said Elizabeth reflectively. 'Do you know if he likes cuff-links, Sherry?'

'I haven't a clue what he likes, except birds – the feathered variety,' snapped Sherry. 'Why can't we live in an area that doesn't suffer from storms?' she wailed, and her friend laughed, divining her meaning without any trouble.

'You *are* in the doldrums,' she said sympathetically. 'Come and do your shopping and we'll get a present for Dee together, if you like,' she offered. They eventually chose a set of cuff-links and a tie-clip to match. 'There, that won't seem so personal if we give him a piece of the set each, if that's what's bothering you,' consoled Elizabeth, with a merry look at Sherry's creased forehead. 'It'll be less awkward than if he gave you a present, and you hadn't one to give back,' she said practically. 'It would spoil Christmas for you.'

Christmas had been spoiled anyhow, thought Sherry, with her uncle away, and suddenly she wished that it was all over and done with, and things were back to normal again, and she could be left alone to get on with the daily routine in her own way. She was sick of complications.

'I'm hungry,' announced Elizabeth. 'We're close to the Royal, let's go in and wait for Dee, it's nearly eleven now.'

'Ooh, my feet ache!' Sherry slid them free of her shoes under cover of the corner table, and sat back in her chair with a sigh of relief: 'Shopping's about the most exhausting pastime I know.'

'At your age nothing should exhaust you,' said a condescending voice from above her head, and Dee dropped into a chair between the two girls, looking infuriatingly fresh and untrodden-on. After battling through three crowded stores in succession, the girls were neither. 'Did you get what you wanted?' he inquired, with a twinkling look at their dishevelled appearance.

'Yes, everything,' said Elizabeth, with a conspiratorial glance at Sherry. 'What about you?' she countered.

'Oh, I got part of what I wanted,' he replied, 'the other half – the important bit – has still to come,' he murmured, and his eyes met Elizabeth's across the table with a warm, intimate glance as of two people who share a secret, a look that startled Sherry out of her tiredness, and made her suddenly wish that she was somewhere else. Their two glances linked and held like the tangible touch of hands reaching out to one another across the table, and Sherry knew unmistakably what it felt like to be redundant. She buried her nose in her coffee cup, wishing she could make some excuse to leave the table. She did not like being made to feel an outsider with her own friend, and a tight feeling of resentment welled up inside her, bringing back the mood of black depression that had first made Elizabeth suggest she took a day off and went shopping.

'Oh, by the way, I saw the Forestry Commission people about your tree while I was in town,' remarked Dee casually, and a smile flicked his firm lips upwards as he was awarded instant attention by the two girls.

'When ...?' they both began at once, and he laughed.

'One at a time! But tomorrow, if that's O.K. with you?' He directed his question to Elizabeth, not to both of them, and Sherry thrust down a quick flash of temper. After all, it was Elizabeth's tree. 'I've got to go and check with the two men responsible, they're working somewhere alongside the Arne, so they should be easy enough to locate.'

'I saw some men at work this morning quite close to the bridge at Battle Pools,' Sherry spoke up. 'You can get along that side of the river easily from the footpath that runs at the back of the garden at home.'

'That's settled, then,' said Dee with satisfaction. 'I can garage the van and walk along to them. I'll give you a ring if there's any alteration to programme,' he promised Elizabeth.

'I seem to be taking up an awful lot of your time.' She looked guilty, and he smiled.

'I'm enjoying it,' he assured her. 'It gives me an

excuse to get out of doors for an hour or two, so it's not entirely selfless,' he confessed.

He would enjoy doing it, for Elizabeth. Anything he did for Sherry always seemed to be done in a mood of exasperation because he didn't trust her to do it properly herself, she thought morosely, and did not hear Elizabeth's question until she repeated herself.

'Who are you daydreaming about?' her friend teased. 'I asked if tomorrow was all right with you as well? You will be coming with us, won't you?' she begged.

'Of course she will,' promised Dee without waiting for Sherry to reply. 'Now, if you two have finished we'd better be getting back so that I can have an early start after lunch. There's a couple of things I want to do before it gets dark.'

He didn't say what the other thing was, and Sherry didn't think to ask him until after they had finished a quick lunch at Arne Cottage.

'I want to finish off a sketch,' he satisfied her curiosity. 'Why not come along with me?' he suggested. His question came out of the blue, and she stared at him in undisguised surprise.

'I hadn't thought . . .' she began, and he interrupted smilingly.

'Neither had I until the Forestry office suggested this morning that I should go along and see the two lumbermen themselves. It's an ideal day for a walk,' he tempted her, 'and the ground by the river shouldn't be boggy in this weather, the frost has been too severe. Why not come along and give yourself a chance to forget the garage for an hour or two?' he coaxed. 'It'll do us both good to get away from work for a bit,' he said truthfully.

'Will I do as I am?' Sherry was still in her driving clothes.

'Yes, but put on some stouter shoes if you've got them.'

She nodded, her driving shoes had soles thin enough to allow her to 'feel' the car, and they would make for cold walking on the frostbitten grass.

'I'll run up and change. Oh, and I'd better ring Ben at the same time and let him know I won't be coming back,' she remembered.

The mechanic was reassuring about the workload for the afternoon.

'There's nothing the other cars can't handle between them,' he told her. 'We've got two drivers in now, waiting for calls.'

'Good, then I can leave you to it,' said Sherry with relief. If they had been busy she would have gone back to work, but common sense told her the value of a break from it, however enthusiastic she might be, and she slipped upstairs and pulled on a pair of stoutly soled ankle boots with a pleasant thrill of playing truant and enjoying it.

'How do we get to the footpath?' Dee was waiting for her in the hall, and nodded approval of her footwear.

'Through the wicket gate at the bottom of the garden. Come on, I'll show you.'

She steered him past the potting shed, and through a screen of laurels to a sturdy wooden gate let into the beech hedge that rustled dead brown leaves against their coats as they pushed past it.

'There's the path. You can just see the line of it from here,' Sherry pointed downhill across the grassland to where a thin line of track showed faintly darker than the rest of the surroundings. It meandered across the dip until it found its level in the shallow valley beside the river bank, and the two of them headed towards it at a tangent, the downhill going hastening their steps until Sherry was breathless.

'Pull up a bit. Use me as a brake,' Dee suggested. 'It's steep here.' He offered his hand, and Sherry reached out and took it, glad of a hold on the dry, slippy grass. Her boot soles were leather, and gave little grip, and the feeling of unsure footing was disconcerting on such a slope.

'I can't see the foresters.'

She scanned the country ahead of them. It was empty of life as far as the slope of a hill half a mile away.

'They're probably over the other side of the rise. If we make towards the roadbridge over Battle Pools I shouldn't think we'd miss them. That's where you said you saw them working this morning.'

He slowed his footsteps to match hers, and soon the path widened and levelled off, following the deeply flowing Arne to within a foot of its edge. Impelled by the magnetism of water, Sherry stopped to watch the current, fascinated as she always was by the ceaseless conversation of the river. On a summer day, when it ran shallow over its bed, the busy gurgle and fuss of its hurrying sounded frivolous and gay, like the chatter of children playing in the sun, but today its steep banks were full to the brim with its winter load, and the current ran strongly, and was quieter, giving its voice a deeper tone as if it had weightier matters to discuss, and be answered by the thin, complaining voice of the wind. Impulsively she stooped and plucked two of the thin reed stems that grew about her feet, and tossed them into the current. Omens, the children called them, and she watched them, interested despite herself, as the play of the water tossed them aimlessly about for a moment or two, then straightened them out as the main current caught and held them closely parallel as it drew them remorselessly along with it towards whatever destination the hurrying water had in mind.

'We used to call them omens.'

Dee's voice was reminiscent, and Sherry flushed as she looked up to find him watching her, a quietly amused look in his eyes, and she wished she had not given way to the sudden impulse to play an almost forgotten childhood game. Then, it had been fun, for carefree children to play guessing games with the river as to who would partner their future, and the next instant forget what it told them as something else of interest caught their lighthearted attention. Now, the pleasure had gone out of such guesses, and in any case, she thought, the river lied. The two reeds still lay close together, cruising steadily on almost out of sight now, but the second one had no name to it, and she had enough difficulties to face until her uncle was back on his feet again, and once more in charge of Manders Motors, without inviting more in the way of romance, she thought bleakly.

Thoughts of the garage brought back the memory of Dee's troubles as well as her own. They were one and the same thing really, she thought ruefully, resuming her pacing, thankful for the comparatively easy walking along the bank.

'Let's hope the weather holds,' she remarked. 'While it stays dry there won't be so much danger of your things in the flat spoiling. Will you move them into store if it gets bad?'

'I'd thought of moving them into store anyhow, as a temporary measure,' he answered. 'It's all very well living over the work premises while you're getting a business on its feet, but it's not much fun when you've got it going,' he confessed. 'Oh, it's comfortable enough,' he answered Sherry's protest, 'and there's plenty of room, but now . . .' He broke off, and Sherry wondered why his living quarters should suddenly seem inadequate to him when they had served him so well up to the present. Perhaps living at Arne Cottage had spoiled him for going back over the garage.

'In any case, I want to expand my working area,' he went on, 'and I couldn't before, without moving premises. Now this has happened I might as well turn it to good account and have the garage restructured more in line with what I shall eventually want. I'd like to get myself a home – a proper one,' he remarked surprisingly, and added with a slight smile, 'particularly one that looks out over the downs and the river the same as Arne Cottage, though of course I shan't want anything quite so big,' he added hastily.

'That's just as well, it's not for sale,' laughed Sherry, 'but it's nice to have a decent view,' she acknowledged. 'You could go birdwatching and sketching any time you wanted from the bottom of your garden if you had a house on this side of the town,' she enlarged, thankful of something to talk about that did not include work, and so spark off the ready antagonism that seemed to lurk so closely beneath the surface whenever that subject came up, and anything to prevent another of the painful silences that arose so frequently between herself and Dee, that he did not seem to want to break, and she did not know how.

'There are usually more houses for sale in the spring,

so I intend to keep a lookout until I find something to suit me. There's no particular urgency yet,' he said indifferently.

So he couldn't be thinking of getting married. Or perhaps he was, but not just yet. So far as Sherry knew he was not engaged, and he didn't seem to have any particular ties in that direction. Certainly since he had been staying at Arne Cottage he hadn't offered to go out in the evenings, which pointed to the fact that he had no regular girlfriend.

'There's a Land-Rover, at the bend of the river.'

She pointed ahead as they breasted the rise, and Dee quickened his step.

'It looks as if they've packed up and are ready for off. 'Hi!' he hailed the vehicle loudly as a puff of exhaust smoke blued from the back. A head popped out of the cab window, and he raised his arms and waved vigorously. 'Stay here, Sherry, I'm going to run and catch them.'

He left her at a swift trot, and Sherry walked on after him along the bank at a leisurely pace. His easy, athletic stride lengthened the distance between them in a remarkably short space of time, and she saw him pull up at the stationary Land-Rover. Evidently what he said was satisfactory to the occupants for after a couple of minutes it moved off and left him standing alone, and he strolled slowly back to Sherry.

'Tomorrow will be all right for them, too,' he told her. 'If it's a decent day it should make quite a pleasant expedition.'

Sherry swallowed her annoyance that he had not bothered to ask her whether she would come or not, casually accepting that she would join the party anyhow, and hoped for Elizabeth's sake that the tree-felling would go off well, since her friend seemed to set a lot of store by it. All her doubts about the strength of Elizabeth's feelings for Andy came back with renewed force, and to stifle them she sought refuge in conversation.

'Where do you want to sketch from? The light won't last too long now up in the plantations.' She glanced at her watch, remembering the black darkness that had enveloped the planting like a cloak the day they went to choose the tree.

'I thought we'd walk to the other side of the road bridge, by the Pools,' he answered, 'if that's not too far for you? I can get all I want from there, and there'll be no need to climb. We can watch the geese come in for the night, as a bonus,' he suggested, and once again Sherry was conscious of his affinity with his surroundings. When they reached the pools he settled himself easily against an outcrop of rocks beside the water and pulled a small sketching pad and pencil from his pocket with the familiarity of someone who had leaned there and sketched before. Sherry would have liked to watch him draw, but refused to invite his teasing by standing on tip-toe to see what was on the page, and he did not offer to lower it and show her.

'I'll show you when it's finished,' was all the satisfaction she got, and with that she had to be content.

The sound of loud splashing, and some indignant squawks turned her feet towards the water's edge, and she watched fascinated while a couple of mallards settled an argument between them, one of them finally floating off with an air of massive dignity as if he was the victor and not the vanquished. She stooped and pulled a small handful of reeds to add to a jar of jasmin she had put on the sideboard at home, and looked up again quickly as Dee called to her from the rock.

'The geese are starting to come in. If you're not too cold, we'll stay and watch.'

Sherry hurried to join him by his rock, her eyes raking the sky above the dark rise of the banked conifers, and she felt a thrill run through her as she made out a distant V-shaped wedge outlined against the lighter heavens. It rapidly transformed itself into individual birds, approaching with slow wing beats, their ponderous bodies and long, snake-like necks curiously graceful in flight. When they were almost overhead the leader dipped towards the surface of the water, and Sherry and Dee had a close-up view as they circled and came in to land, their forward thrusting webbed feet acting as perfect, natural brakes against the solid resistance of the water, each foot cleaving a fine line of spray that gleamed briefly, jewel-like, in the fading light, until one by one the birds settled, floating quietly, talking among themselves with small, contented murmurings.

Others followed quickly until the air seemed full of the sigh of wings and the faint hissing splash as they water-skated to rest, and then the sky was empty of life, cleared of its evening traffic that was now neatly parked for the night, looking smaller and more compact on the water than they had in the air, with their long necks retracted, like a fleet of miniature submarines with their periscopes raised against any sign of danger from the shore. With their coming the wild, deserted place took on a warmly peopled look, and Dee's voice sounded satisfied when he spoke.

'They're home.' He raised himself slowly away from the rock and put his hand on Sherry's shoulder, drawing her off the cold hardness of it that unnoticed had struck a chill through her warm jacket, so that she shivered, glad of the prospect of a brisk walk back to Arne Cottage. 'We'll make for home, too, you're cold. I shouldn't have kept you here so long.'

His voice was concerned, and Sherry shook her head emphatically.

'I'm glad we came. I've – enjoyed it.'

Enjoy seemed an inadequate word, she thought, for the deep response of feeling that had unexpectedly welled inside her at the sight of the wild, flighting flock, and the satisfaction that she knew was shared by Dee from the quiet finality of his 'they're home'. Perhaps that was what he wanted, when he spoke of getting a house for himself with an outlook over the downs and the river the same as Arne Cottage enjoyed. Maybe he, too, wanted a home, rather than just living quarters such as he had got now, however luxuriously appointed they were. Perhaps he longed for a place that he could truly know as his own, and bring to warm life, as the geese had brought to life the cold, silent waters of the mere. Somewhere that he could people, for a home must have either people or memories to warm it, and people came first, at the young fresh beginning of life, as voices had to sound before their echo could be heard.

Sherry wondered again if Dee had marriage in mind, and wondered still further why the thought of Elizabeth should come to her so persistently every time she thought of Dee.

CHAPTER NINE

DESPITE her vexation with Dee, Sherry found herself looking forward to the tree-felling expedition the next morning.

Her first instinct had been to refuse to go, and carry on to work as usual in defiance of his casual acceptance that she would join the party, but when the sun rose on a clear sky that shone coldly blue above them, her resolution melted, and she wrapped herself in an old brown corduroy trouser suit and joined him in the cab of his lorry, feeling the same thrill of expectation that she used to feel as a small girl on unexpected outings with her uncle. She wriggled back on the hard bench seat, that was more functional than comfortable, and Dee started the engine into life.

'Oh, wait a minute!'

She pushed herself forward hurriedly to her feet, which had been easily a couple of inches from the floor, and Dee slipped the gear back into neutral.

'Now what?' He looked resigned.

'I've forgotten a basket for the cones.' She would bring enough home with her for the fire tonight, they would make the room smell nice. She reached out for the door handle, which she had discovered was stiff and needed two hands to turn it.

'Don't bother to get out,' Dee halted her. 'I've got a clean hessian sack tucked in the side of the seat. You can use that, it's only a small one,' he told her. He reached down beside him and brought out a straw-coloured roll and handed it over, and Sherry tucked it behind her; it would serve as a cushion until they got to the plantation. The new, pale-coloured fibres gave off a faint musty smell redolent of a granary – or a prison workshop, she thought with a smile.

'Settled now?' Dee looked across at her, and his own face lightened at her expression. 'Are you looking forward to it?'

'Mmm,' Sherry nodded, happy to forget the tension that had built up between them, if it was only for one morning. 'Where are we meeting Elizabeth?'

'At the Lomax works. There's room in the cab for the three of us if you squash up a bit, and the Forestry Commission men will take you back to the factory canteen in their van. They promised to give us a hand erecting the tree, to make sure it was standing safely,' he explained.

'Can't we travel back with you?' Sherry felt curiously disappointed. It would have been nice to ride back with the tree, like riding back on the last wagon from the hayfields, she thought, remembering long-ago farm holidays with her uncle.

'No, you can't,' Dee was adamant. 'One of the Commission men will ride back with me once we've got the tree aboard. You and Elizabeth can travel safely back on the van with the other.'

'Safely back? Is there any danger, Dee?' Sherry thought of the steep tracks to the plantation that they had climbed previously, and her heart missed a beat. If the lorry tipped . . .

'No, of course not,' he laughed at her troubled expression. 'I told you, we shall come from the other side of the plantation where the slope is a lot gentler. I meant safely out of my way,' he told her firmly. 'Once I've got the tree aboard I want someone in the cab with me who knows the ropes,' he told her.

His argument was logical enough, but nevertheless Sherry felt a pang of regret. She would have liked to help, though she realized that her own slight stature would not compare with that of a brawny woodsman, even enthusiasm could not make up for that. The prospect of a change of transport did not seem to bother Elizabeth.

'Our turn will come when the tree is up,' she consoled Sherry. 'We'll be in charge of the decorating. Shuffle over a bit,' she commanded, hauling herself up into the cab and preparing to slam the door behind her.

'Come closer to me.' Dee put his arm round Sherry and pulled her across the shiny leather seat towards him. His muscles felt hard underneath the thin waterproof of his windcheater, and he held her close against him until Elizabeth was settled, then he let her go. 'Keep your feet out of the way of the gear lever,' he told her. 'We shan't be long before we're at the plantation, you won't have time to get too uncomfortable.'

Sherry hitched her right foot underneath her, and put both her arms round her knee. It made a comfortable rest for her chin, and having her heel on the seat gave her a greater feeling of security, since her other foot dangled well above the floor.

'Don't brake suddenly,' she warned him, 'or you'll have me through the windscreen.'

'Here, put your feet on this.' He reached down beside him again and brought out a shallow wooden tray. 'It's a fish box,' he explained, and Sherry sniffed.

'You're telling me!' she retorted disparagingly. 'I

prefer the sack!'

Nevertheless she took it from him and wedged it in front of her, out of the way of his gear lever, making a firm footrest that held her comfortably on the wide seat.

'Lorries don't boast safety belts,' said Dee regretfully, 'but we shall soon be off the road. Here we are,' he swung the lorry wide through an opening in a drystone wall, and Sherry saw the dark blur of the plantation far away from them to their right.

'It looks a good way off.' From this distance the three meres of Battle Pools were merged into one single sheet of water, a narrow silver wedge in the valley that gave no hint of its real size to unfamiliar eyes.

'I told you, this way the slope is a lot longer, but it's gentler, better for the vehicle and safer for us.' As he spoke Dee juggled with the levers in front of him, engaging the extra set of low gears with which the lorry was provided, and started the long, slow crawl up the rough plantation track. 'Most of this has still got to be cleared and planted,' he remarked conversationally, 'but as it is now it makes excellent birdwatching cover.' He waved his hand at the tangle of scrub and mixed deciduous spinney that confronted them, fringing the bottom of the hill with a brown girdle of bare winter branches, broken here and there by the dark green of holly. A Land-Rover was pulled up close under the shelter of the trees, parked with its face to the road, but no occupants were visible. 'That belongs to the Commission men,' said Dee. 'It looks as if they've decided to walk up ahead of us.'

'All that way, uphill?' Sherry pointed ahead, appalled.

'It's no distance to them, they're used to it,' laughed

Dee, amused at her horrified expression. 'You climbed a much steeper slope a week ago. Remember?'

'Vividly!' She gazed with interest at the approaching dark green cover on the hill, intrigued by the new planting of baby trees no more than a foot high, miniatures of the serried ranks of giants above them, their lighter-tipped fronds giving them a curiously innocent look.

'Aren't they sweet? I'd love to take one home,' coveted Elizabeth aloud.

'And find in a few years' time you've got something that's taken over the garden,' cautioned Dee. 'Leave them where they belong, you can always walk up here and enjoy them.'

That's what Dee did, thought Sherry with quick perception. Walked up here and enjoyed the trees. And all that went with them – the birds, and the solitude, and the myriad sights and sounds of a semi-wilderness. He belonged here, as much as the foresters who stood waiting for them at the intersection of two rides, on a broad flat piece of grass that Sherry recognized as the spot where Dee had chosen the tree a week ago. She could see the white flash of the chalk mark he had made on its trunk. The two foresters themselves were not what Sherry expected. Although they were anything but short, standing as tall as Dee himself, they were built with a wiry slimness that was the opposite to the village-smithy image she had expected. She said as much in a disappointed voice, and Dee laughed out loud.

'Time doesn't stand still, even in the forests,' he told her. 'There isn't so much call for sheer muscle power now. The equipment they use is as up-to-date as anything Elizabeth's father has got in his factory. The days when men did all the hefting themselves have gone,' he assured her. 'There's still some done by hand, of course, but most of the hard slog is taken out of it by machinery. Where do you intend to drop it?' he called, sticking his head through the cab window as the lorry whined to a halt on the small plateau.

'Across the intersection, I reckon.' The older of the two men indicated a diagonal line with a sweep of his hand. 'If you'll draw your vehicle up about there, Mr. Lawrence,' he nodded in the same direction, 'we can load it fairly easily from where it comes down.'

'How on earth do they know where it's going to fall?' whispered Elizabeth.

'That's where the skill comes in.' Dee overheard her remark. 'Let's park up there and get out, we can watch from somewhere on the ride above them.'

'Aren't you going to help?' Elizabeth looked surprised.

'I'm better out of their way,' retorted Dee. 'They know what they're doing, and they won't want me under their feet while they're doing it.'

'I'm glad he admits it,' thought Sherry, with a feeling of satisfaction that she was not the only one who was wanted safely out of someone else's way. She slid out of the cab after Elizabeth, and smiled a thank-you as one of the foresters caught her and steadied her on her feet as she landed.

'You'll have to carry a stepladder about with you,' jested Dee.' 'The van's too high for you to jump out of safely, and this cab is even higher.'

Sherry gave him a withering look. She would have liked to make a withering reply, but held her tongue in front of the two strangers, reluctant to spoil the day they had all looked forward to.

'How do you know where the tree is going to drop?' She felt distinctly uneasy, for the sake of the lorry. It looked a lot too close for comfort to where the forester had said the tree would fall. Dee had lost the roof off his premises, it would be disastrous if he lost his lorry as well.

'Don't worry, miss, I reckon to be able to drop a tree on a matchstick,' grinned the man.

'On a crossways matchstick,' retorted his companion crushingly. 'I can drop one on a matchstick lying the same way as the tree,' he boasted, and Dee laughed and took the girls' arms.

'Come on, let's walk on up,' he commanded. 'Once these two start vying with one another, there's no knowing when they'll stop. Have you got your sack?' he inquired, and Sherry turned back towards the lorry.

'No, I forgot, it's still on the back of the seat.'

'I'll get it, you two start walking up.' He went back towards the cab, and the younger of the two foresters paced beside them.

'I should stand here, if I were you, miss. You'll be able to see what we're doing, and . . .' He stopped.

'And be safely out of your way,' Elizabeth finished for him smilingly. 'It was kind of you to do the job for us,' she thanked him.

'Our pleasure, miss. We all know about the children's party you give at Christmas,' he assured her. 'My mate's two youngsters are going, so we've got a vested interest, so to speak.'

He nodded in a friendly fashion and strolled away to join his companion, and Dee shook out the sack and held it towards Sherry.

'You'd best have it, in case I forget and take it back

with me.' He handed it over, and spun round as the thud of an axe riveted their attention on the chosen tree. The sun glinted on the gleaming blade as the younger forester swung it high, and brought it down again with skilled precision, and Sherry saw a pale gash appear low down on the trunk. The man with the axe straightened and felt in his pocket, a voluminous affair that looked as if it carried an assortment of useful odds and ends, and his hand reappeared with a wedge. He inserted the thin end in the gash, using the back of his axe to firm it into position, and reached out for something that looked like a mechanical hedge-cutter, lying on the ground beside him.

'It's a motorized saw,' explained Dee. So that was the modern machinery, thought Sherry.

'Very sensible,' approved Elizabeth, 'think of the effort it must save.'

'Yes, but it spoils the image,' countered Dee with an amused look at Sherry's rapt expression. 'Powered saws don't develop brawny muscles.'

Sherry made a face at him, refusing to be drawn, and the staccato splutter of the small engine would have drowned her words anyway. The Forestry man glanced once in the direction where he wanted the tree to fall, gave the wedge a last tap, and inserted the blade of his saw in the axe gash. Immediately the noise of the engine conceded first place to a rising, high-pitched scream as the blade of the saw cut into the living wood, and Sherry saw the tree shudder right to its tip. She caught her breath sharply. It was like watching a person being executed. Impulsively, she took a step towards the tree, and felt Dee's fingers close about her arm.

'I know.' His voice was low, oddly sympathetic. 'But

think of the children, how disappointed they'd be on Boxing Day with no tree for their party.' He moved down until he was standing just behind her, and she looked up and back, into his face. Until now his habitual expression when she was with him was either angry or teasing, but now it was neither. His vivid eyes met hers with a quiet acceptance of shared feelings – a mutual knowing, with no need of words between them, Sherry let her breath out in a sigh, and Dee released her arm and put both his hands on her shoulders, drawing her gently back to lean against him. His tall figure sheltered her slight frame from the bite of the wind that whistled along the ride, and she rested against him, grateful for the comparative warmth.

The thin wail of the saw stopped abruptly, and the two foresters stepped back. For a second, nothing happened. It was as if the whole forest waited, holding its breath. Then slowly, the graceful, tapering tip of the tree trembled and leaned in the direction the forester had chosen. Gradually at first, as if it was reluctant to part from the stem that had supported it for so long, and then swiftly as the force of the wedge tilted it inexorably in the one direction, the green tip described an arc against the bright sky, and the tree crashed on to the intersection of the two rides, bouncing once or twice on its springy branches before finally settling to rest, as if accepting its fate.

'What a shame!'

Elizabeth's voice was subdued, all the thrill of watching the tree-felling gone from her face, and the man holding the saw glanced towards her.

'They're grown for use, Miss Lomax,' he told her practically. 'And they've got to be felled before they can be used. You can't have your children's party on the hill, now, can you?' he tried to cheer her woe-begone expression.

'No-o. But I didn't think it would make me feel quite such a – a – murderer!'

Dee looked at her, and his own face was sober.

'Let's get moving and dispose of the body, then,' he said bracingly. 'We've got to get it onto the lorry, and then down to your works canteen,' he reminded her, 'and it's nearly eleven now. If you want it erected, and decorated by teatime . . .'

'You said you'd bring a block and tackle along with you,' Mr. Lawrence?' hinted the older of the two men.

'I've got it in the back of the lorry. Stay where you are for a minute,' he called to the two girls, and strode away towards where his vehicle stood, parked now parallel with the fallen tree. He vaulted lightly up into the back and rummaged around on the floor, and Sherry heard the rattle of equipment, and something that sounded like the clank of a chain. It was a cold, hard, sound, and she shivered.

'Are you cold?' asked Elizabeth, and Sherry shook her head. She could not explain even to herself what had caused the shiver.

Dee unhitched the backboard of the lorry and let it swing down, pushing his equipment out on to the ground where it fell with a noisy clatter.

'Why don't you go and gather your cones?' he suggested, overhearing Elizabeth's remark. 'It would keep you warm, and there's nothing much to see here now, we've only got to dispose of the body,' he teased, with a sly look at the fair-haired girl, and Sherry realized she was still holding the sack in her hands.

'Why not start to walk down towards the van, miss?'

The younger forester spoke up. 'You'll be coming back with me,' he reminded them, 'and I'll catch you up as soon as we've got the tree roped on the lorry.'

'We'll wait for you down there,' his companion butted in. 'The boss said we've to cut a bunch or two of holly, and some of the mistletoe that's growing on that willow down by the marshy bit. It'll all add a bit to your decorations, miss,' he spoke to Elizabeth. 'There's nothing like a few holly-berries to brighten up a room for a party.'

'That will be lovely.' Elizabeth's voice had got its enthusiasm back, and she turned to Sherry. 'Shall we leave them to it, and pick up our cones on the way? We can always drag the sack behind us down the slope if it gets too heavy to carry.'

'A good idea. Come on!' Sherry grasped her friend's hand and started off hurriedly down hill, suddenly urgent to be gone. She had had enough of tree-felling, and surrendered without a struggle to an overwhelming panic urge for flight that took possession of her, seeking in swift movement to avoid the question that arose in her mind, of what she was fleeing from.

Was it from the sight of the stricken tree, lying still and silent at their feet where so short a time before it had raised proud arms towards the skies? Or was it from the remembered feel of two strong hands grasping her shoulders, with a masterful yet gentle touch that seemed to burn right through the soft corduroy of her jacket, and send a strange, thrilling warmth through her veins such as she had never felt before.

CHAPTER TEN

SHERRY slackened her pace only when a bend in the track hid the fallen tree, and the men working on it, from their sight.

'Phew! That's better!' exclaimed Elizabeth breathlessly. 'I don't like tree-felling either,' she admitted, clearly blaming Sherry's haste on her reaction when the foresters claimed the fir.

'Sorry, I didn't mean to make you run, but it's downhill as well,' Sherry's excuse sounded lame even in her own ears, but it seemed to satisfy her friend, and she felt guilty. The two had always confided in one another, but somehow she couldn't bring herself to speak, even to Elizabeth, of the powerful upsurge of emotion that had descended on her out of the blue, thrilling through her nerves with a bewildering mixture of ice and fire that made her want to sing and cry at the same time, and made her strangely afraid. Her head buzzed with questions and answers, questions that thrust themselves on her unwilling consciousness until her weakened resistance had no power to push them away, and answers that brought a bitter-sweet torment that did nothing to ease the odd little ache in the region of her heart, that she had wondered about often during the last few days, and now she knew the reason for it. And felt no happier for the knowing.

'Here's a beauty. And another. Bring the sack over, there's lots of cones here,' called Elizabeth, busy on her knees on the soft floor of pine needles under the trees.

'Mmm? Oh, the sack ...' Sherry came back to her surroundings with a jolt, and felt faintly surprised that they still looked the same. She felt as if she had been on a long, long journey, and would not have questioned it if she had found Elizabeth's fair head had taken on some streaks of grey, so much time seemed to have elapsed since she started out. Her friend gave her a hard look under pretext of displaying the cones.

'Some of these might do for decorating the tree,' she suggested. 'I've got a tin of that silver-spray stuff that would colour the tips nicely.'

'Let's keep the best ones on the top of the sack then, we can put the little ones in the bottom for the fire.'

Sherry discovered that she could still speak and act rationally, despite the cyclonic effect of her feelings inside her, and even enjoy picking up the cones. The tangy odour of the forest and the rough, dry feel of the cones in her hand seemed more sharply defined, some-how, as did the outlines of the branches etched against the sky above them. Was this what love did? she won-dered. Made one more aware? If so, it could have its compensations, though shrinking from the turmoil of her own feelings she felt it to be the only one.

Alternately picking up cones and strolling on, they were a good half-way down the hill when the lorry passed them with a friendly hoot, and rattled on its way ahead of them, the tree in the back securely roped, its branches moving at the behest of the bouncing vehicle as if it, too, waved to them as it passed. Momentarily the long vehicle slowed, and the young forester dropped off the back on to the grass of the ride. He turned and gave two hard thumps with his fist on the wooden side as a signal for Dee to drive on, and cheer-fully joined the girls, with a pleased look on his face as if he found his out-of-the-way duty very much to his liking.

'You've done well,' he approved, indicating their filled sack, which by now was heavy enough to be dragged, with Sherry and Elizabeth holding a corner each. 'Let me take it, you've done your stint,' he smiled, and with humiliating ease he swung it nonchalantly over his shoulder as if he was used to carrying a duffel bag, and Sherry wondered if he had ever been in the Navy. Despite the biting wind, his sweater sleeves were pushed up to his elbows, showing the dark stain of tattoo marks under his mahogany skin.

'The others will wait for us at the bottom,' he told them, 'you can choose your holly and mistletoe then, and take the lot back with you in the lorry.'

'Let's hope they're easier to choose than the tree was,' retorted Elizabeth fervently.

'Have the sprays with the most berries on,' suggested Dee, overhearing her remark as they joined him. 'That will make your choice a lot easier.'

'It always seems such a shame to deprive the birds.' Elizabeth gazed longingly at the rambling bush confronting them. The dark, spiky leaves shone as if they had been polished, and the cold winter sunshine penetrated the bare branches of the scrub oak spinney as easily as if they were not there, and made bright jewels of the vivid berries hanging in scarlet clusters to its very tip.

'They say it means a hard winter when the trees are loaded like this.'

'It means conditions were right when the bush flowered in the spring,' one of the foresters said practically, and Dee shook his head at him.

'Leave the girls their bit of folklore,' he admonished,

'even if it isn't true they like fairy tales at Christmas time.'

'Wrong again!' thought Sherry, and felt shocked by a swift bitterness. Why wouldn't Dee treat her as a grown-up? She had grown up, painfully and very swiftly in the last hour, she thought, though Dee was not to know that. Must not know it. She felt frightened at the very possibility. She could not bear him to tease her about this one thing. She had not got used to it herself yet, let alone accepted it, and to have it aired and probably scorned by him, or worse still laughed at, would be intolerable.

'Gather the berried bits and put them in water so that the berries won't wither. That way you can have your decorations, and toss the sprays out for the birds afterwards,' he suggested to Elizabeth. 'The birds won't say no to them, in this temperature,' he assured her.

'I hadn't thought of that.' Patently relieved, Elizabeth pointed to a heavily berried spray at the top of the bush. 'I'd love that one,' she said hopefully, and the forester, catching Dee's amused expression, made no attempt to hide his own broad smile.

'Just like my missus!' he exclaimed. 'When we're blackberrying it's the same, she always wants the berries that are out of reach.' Nevertheless he good-humouredly drew the branch down and clipped off the spray, and handed it to Elizabeth, who had the grace to look ashamed and obligingly chose her other sprays from within his not inconsiderable reach.

'Give them to me,' Dee over-ruled her protest when he attempted to relieve her of her burden. 'I know they're nice to hold, but you've got the mistletoe to get yet, and you can't carry both. Besides, it's a rough walk

146

to the willow trees.'

He stowed the holly safely in the lorry beside the tree and took the girls by an arm each, steering them after the two foresters who turned off along a seemingly inaccessible track, clearing the undergrowth with their forceful stride to make the walking easier for the two girls.

'Watch your step,' he cautioned as the trees thinned and the thicket gave way to clumps of rush. 'It's swampy here. Follow the men across in Indian file, and you won't get your feet wet.'

'Is there a path?' Sherry sounded dubious. After her experience of jumping the runnels on their previous visit to the plantation she did not relish leaping from clump to clump here. She had not got the stride of the foresters, who both seemed as sure-footed as cats in their chosen environment, as indeed was Dee, marking him as a man who was as at home there as they.

'Yes, it's quite firm, you won't get your feet wet today,' he consoled her. 'The frost last night was too severe for the ground to be soft.'

Nevertheless she was conscious of him keeping close behind her, and once when the going deteriorated he put out a steadying hand, but when they neared the willow trees and saw several large bunches of mistletoe hanging from their gnarled arms, both the girls forgot the roughness of the track and hurried behind the foresters.

'You'll have to catch it, miss.' The older of the two men eyed Elizabeth gravely.

'Very well.' She stepped forward willingly to help, then hesitated. 'I'm not very good at catching.' She glanced in the direction of the other man. 'Perhaps . . .?'

'Not me, miss! I'm staying out of this!' he exclaimed, with such fervour that she shot him a puzzled look, obviously wondering at his reluctance where before he had been so helpful.

'Oh well.' Philosophically she stood underneath the branch and held out her arms. Fortunately it was low enough to make it a straight drop for the yellow-green bunch hanging above her, and with a quick nick of his axe-head the man severed it from its host, and it was safely in its new owner's hands. She turned a delighted face to Dee.

'I'll make a good cricketer yet,' she cried.

'I reckon you've got another career mapped out for you, miss, according to the way you caught that bunch,' said the younger man dryly.

'Why, what's that got to do with it? Catching this was just pure luck,' she retorted honestly. 'I'm a terrible butter-fingers normally.'

'Not where it counts,' replied the forester. 'Where we come from the one who catches the mistletoe gets married within the year.'

'So that's why you wouldn't?'

'Not me, miss! I'm all for staying single for a bit longer,' he declared with a grin, which broadened as Elizabeth realized the personal implications of her catch, and flushed a rosy red.

'And you accuse us of liking fairy tales!' she exclaimed to Dee, shaking her head at him, but her glance, as their eyes met, was warm, the same close, intimate look that they had exchanged across the coffee cups on the day they all went shopping, thought Sherry. A look as of two people who share a precious secret. Momentarily a small, desolate feeling overcame her, as if she and the foresters were not really there at all.

'Some fairy tales come true.' Dee's voice was quiet, with an underlying seriousness in his tone that deepened Elizabeth's colour, and his eyes smiled warmly across at her.

'They're in love!'

Sherry's throat suddenly went dry, and she swallowed quickly, and found an unexpected lump there that had not been in evidence before. Dee and Elizabeth. Elizabeth and Dee. Why hadn't she seen it before? she wondered, but perhaps, subconsciously, she had, and had failed to recognize the signs. When Dee had spoken to her of his wish to buy a house, she remembered that Elizabeth's face had persisted in invading her thoughts. She had wondered why, at the time, but it seemed obvious now. Poor Andy! A quick spasm of sympathy caught at her for the likeable young Canadian. His feelings would reflect her own, she knew, and hers were miserable enough, goodness knows. If this was love, she thought ruefully, it didn't make for the happiness the romantics would have people believe. Her thoughts ran round and round in bewilderment. Why did it have to be Dee? A few short hours ago and she would not have cared, but now? Now, she cared very much, she admitted honestly, and it was no good pretending otherwise, at least not to herself. The others must not suspect. The thought stiffened her courage, and brought a flow of life back to limbs that had begun to tremble.

'Are you going to catch a bunch, miss?'

The forester spoke to her twice before she heard him, and hurriedly she shook her head.

'Maybe I'm like you, and want to stay free for a bit longer,' she refused, using the word free deliberately, and not single, as he had, trying to make it sound as if she had no wish to get married. She hadn't, to anyone but Dee, she thought miserably, and it was too late to wish for that now.

'How about you having a try, Mr. Lawrence,' asked the man jokingly, 'you'll need another bunch for the ladies to take home to decorate the house with. It's a shame to waste it all on a children's party,' he added meaningly.

'Anything to oblige.' Dee reached out a casual arm and stayed the falling bunch as it left the axe. It was a much smaller one this time, one or two good sprays, but adequate for Elizabeth and Sherry to share for their respective homes. Dee looked at it reflectively for a moment as it rested in his hands, then he spun round suddenly and tossed it in Sherry's direction. 'Catch!' he called, unexpectedly. She had not realized his intention, and was caught offguard, but instinctively she grabbed at the bunch rather than let it fall to the ground, and managed to catch the nearest twig. She grasped it hastily, and her fingers held, allowing her to cradle it safely in both hands. Startled out of her reverie the sudden action on Dee's part started a prick of tears behind her eyes, and she blinked hastily.

'It looks as if I might be a bridesmaid.'

She turned to Elizabeth and held up her smaller bunch triumphantly, with a smile that felt stiff on her face, her whole body felt rigid with the effort of self-control.

'That's a foregone conclusion.' Her friend linked her arm through Sherry's affectionately. 'You must be my chief bridesmaid. They always marry the best man,' she added teasingly.

'Perhaps I shall be driving you to your wedding instead.' It seemed a silly thing to say, intruding business into their friendship, a thing they had both been careful never to do before, but it was the first thing that came into her head, a safe, familiar ground in a world that had suddenly become insecure. It could provide her with a way out too, she thought, a way of attending the wedding and serving her friend without actually walking behind her up the aisle, and taking her to marry Dee. For how could she stand calmly through the ceremony, and watch her best friend vow to love, honour and obey until death did them part the man whom she herself loved? Sherry's normal supply of resolute courage failed her at the thought, and her desperate mind grasped at the only possible alternative, but Elizabeth was adamant.

'Not likely! You'll have the order for the cars, of course,' she told her, 'but let Syd do your driving that day. I shall want you close to me, to give me courage.'

Courage.

It was the one thing that Sherry felt she no longer possessed. Her entire world seemed suddenly to have turned completely upside down, the quiet, secure routine of home and work had become an onerous responsibility, and her innermost feelings, that had never before been so deeply stirred, had flowered into fragile life in a bleak, inhospitable climate and found their blooming inappropriate in both time and direction, so that they would have to be left to wither, slowly and painfully, for lack of a responsive love to nourish them.

Sherry turned back along the path behind Elizabeth, hardly aware of where she put her feet, conscious only of Dee coming close behind her, and willing herself not to stumble so that he should not reach out to steady her, as she guessed he would. She shrank from the contact of his touch, afraid of revealing her feelings that she was desperately anxious to control before she had to come face to face with him when the path ended. Having to walk in single file helped; each one of her companions had to concentrate on where they were putting their own feet on the uneven path, and it afforded her a momentary isolation for which she was grateful. A sharp, scolding trill from the nearby thickets made her raise her head, startled by the loudness of the unknown's voice, and she searched the undergrowth, looking for the origin of the sound.

'That's a wren, he's in the brush somewhere up there.'

Dee pointed to a tangle of greenery away to their left.

'I thought it sounded much closer, it's so loud. Surely it's a bigger bird than a wren, to make such a noise?'

'Mr. Lawrence is right, miss,' commented one of the men from in front of them, 'it's a wren all right. Nature often gives the littlest ones the loudest voices,' he said amusedly. 'It helps them to assert their rights when they're only half the size of the others.'

'That must be why Sherry's got auburn hair,' laughed Dee. 'She's only pint-sized, but she makes a formidable opponent,' he teased.

Sherry turned and glared at him, perversely grateful now for his teasing, for vexation stiffened her morale and gave her the courage she needed to control her emotions so that they did not show in her face. She was not so sure that she could control the reflection of her feelings in her eyes when she looked at Dee, so she carefully averted her face, glad now that she and Elizabeth were travelling back in the Land-Rover with the younger forester, and not in the lorry along with Dee as she had originally hoped.

The journey to the Lomax works seemed all too short, her reluctance to face Dee willing the time to drag on. Her quick spark of temper at his teasing had given her back a shaky self-control, but she did not feel that she could trust it too far, and hoped the two men would remain with them for the afternoon. Her hopes on this score were soon dashed by the speed with which they erected the tree, this time enlisting Dee's help, and that of Andy who had wandered into the canteen with Hereward Lomax to view their choice, and to see how they were getting on.

'I hope he doesn't ruin his clothes.' Elizabeth eyed the impeccably tailored Canadian with a twinge of conscience that was only slightly relieved when he doffed his jacket to reveal a perfectly laundered white shirt.

'It's all in a good cause,' he assured her, joining in with boyish enjoyment while the foresters manipulated pulleys and ropes, and it seemed that in minutes the recumbent fir was vertical again, safely secured to the roof struts, and to stout wooden battens at its base.

'I reckon that'll do, Mr. Lomax.'

The senior forester began collecting his tackle, and the two men disappeared along with Elizabeth's father towards the good lunch which he had arranged for them.

'Let's have ours down here, unless any of you are particularly hungry?' suggested Elizabeth, reluctant to leave her tree now that it was up. Nobody was, the men opting for coffee and sandwiches and getting on with the job, while Sherry felt that food would choke her. Elizabeth herself was too excited to want to eat, and the others evidently thought Sherry's reluctance to partake of anything but the coffee stemmed from the same reason.

The two girls rose to their feet eagerly, though driven by different reactions, when two of the workmen from the factory arrived in the canteen with some lightweight scaffolding, and soon the tall tree was surrounded by a firmly fixed mixture of platforms and ladders that would make their task of dressing the tree to its top a lot easier, as well as safer. Elizabeth turned to a large brown cardboard carton standing by the wall, and started to open it with hurried fingers.

'These are the decorations I got the other day. Let's start now, if you've finished eating.'

Sherry joined her, glad of an excuse to give up the pretence of swallowing food, and Hereward Lomax smiled indulgently as he returned to the canteen and surveyed the mass of tinsel and coloured balls, and all the paraphernalia of Christmas decorations with which they were surrounded.

'Remember to leave room for the electric lights,' he admonished them. 'The electricians will want some part of the branches to fix them to,' he warned.

'We'll leave them their share,' his daughter promised. 'Thank goodness Dee was able to let us have his lorry,' she exclaimed. 'I'd forgotten all about the party when we let our own transport section go.'

'Talking of transport,' Hereward Lomax turned to Dee, who was dutifully handing up bunches of silver bells to the two girls, 'your quote got through our financial people all right. Yours too, Sherry,' he looked up to where she stood on the lowest platform. 'The quote we had from Saville Hire was unrealistically high, so you really had no competition,' he told her. 'It was virtually a clear field. You'll each get a contract from us in the New Year,' he promised.

'Oh, Sherry, I'm so glad,' cried Elizabeth. 'Think how pleased your uncle will be!'

He'd be delighted, Sherry knew. And so ought she to be, as well, but Hereward Lomax's news left her with a strangely flat feeling. The thing that had mattered to her so much a week ago, to prove her ability to run the business on her own, now seemed strangely unimportant, and her words of thanks to her friend's father sounded hollow and insincere. His comment 'you really had no competition' sent a stab through her heart. She had competition, in the thing that mattered to her more than anything else in the world, and her competitor was her best friend. Any jubilation she would have ordinarily felt in gaining the Lomax contract for her uncle died stillborn, and a choking feeling of tears caught at her throat. She hadn't had a clear field in this, the race was already over and won, and while she, Sherry, had lagged behind, Elizabeth had taken the prize.

'Don't look like that about it Sherry, it's no one's fault but their own.'

Sherry looked up at him through a haze. Whose fault did he mean, Dee's and Elizabeth's? It wasn't their fault that they loved one another, she thought numbly, it was only her misfortune.

'If Saville Hire want business, they must quote reasonable prices,' went on Hereward Lomax firmly. 'You needn't look so sorry for them. You're too kind-hearted to run a business,' he scolded, in a tone very like her uncle's when he had declared 'it's no job for a woman'. Silently she agreed with them both. A month ago she would just as vehemently have denied it, but the last revealing weeks had taught her more than the running of a business, she thought. They had taught her about herself. She was still capable of running Manders Motors, capable and confident, and she would continue to do so until her uncle could take over again, but now she knew without any doubt that her heart was not set on a business career, it had exerted a stronger will of its own that had no leaning towards commerce, seeking of its own instinct a life that demanded different strengths and different responsibilities, just as onerous, but nearer to its own desires, that seemed unlikely to ever be fulfilled now, she thought bleakly.

'There's only this left.' Dee searched the bottom of the cardboard box and held out a long paper packet. Elizabeth reached down and took it from his hands.

'It's the fairy. You didn't see it when we were shopping, did you?' she asked Sherry, unwrapping the covering to reveal a doll in long, white clothes.

'It looks more like a bride.' Sherry eyed it doubtfully.

'It is, but they hadn't got a fairy left, so I bought this as the next best thing. You don't think they'll notice it isn't a fairy, when it's on top of the tree?' She looked anxious.

'Of course they won't,' Dee answered her robustly. 'Give it to me and I'll fix it on for you.' He took it from her hands and climbed up to the top of the scaffolding. 'There, the children won't be able to tell the difference,' he assured her, regaining floor level and surveying his handiwork critically.

Sherry gazed upwards, her eyes wistful.

'Her dress is lovely.'

'I'd rather have cream than white when I get married.' Elizabeth's voice was dreamy. 'I'll wear Mother's wedding dress, it's cream lace. And with your hair,' she turned to Sherry, warming to the subject, 'you could wear a pale coffee colour, just a bit deeper than my dress, and carry flame-coloured freesias,' she enthused.

'That would be lovely.' Automatically Sherry agreed, but her mind felt numb. The combination of colours that Elizabeth had mentioned would be both rich and unusual, but inside her she felt that grey would be a better choice of colour for her own dress. The deep, softly shaded grey of clouds that come with drifting rain from skies that mourn, would be more appropriate to her own feelings than the warm, rich colour and bright flowers that her friend had in mind.

CHAPTER ELEVEN

Sherry tried to instil some enthusiasm into her voice when she phoned her uncle about the contract that evening, and for a while she caught a momentary reflection of his pleasure as he voiced his congratulations, though her sense of achievement was short-lived, and swiftly gave way to the weight of depression that had settled on her spirits like a cloud. Humphrey Manders was eager to know the details, and she gave him all she had, thankful that she had some news to take his attention, and so head off his usual affectionate questions as to how things were with her. Her uncle had a keen perception that was not lessened by distance, and she did not want him to sense her own depression, and perhaps worry about it.

He was obviously champing at the bit and keen to be back at the garage, which was a good sign in itself thought Sherry with relief, enlarging on Elizabeth's Christmas tree to fill in the rest of her evening chat with him. She did not mention Elizabeth and Dee; there had been nothing openly spoken of yet anyway, and by the time her uncle learned the news she would have control of her own feelings so that he would not guess what it meant to her.

The two days of Christmas, that had always flown for Sherry, now seemed to stretch before her like an empty void, with only the open-air carol service round the Christmas tree at the Castle Chapel on Christmas Eve to lighten the long, painful hours that must be lived in Dee's company, the thought of which had now become an almost unbearable strain. She could make a flying visit to Devon to see her uncle and aunt, but she knew Polly would never forgive her such a breach of good manners if she quit the house while Dee was their guest – her guest, since her uncle was away. She quailed at the thought of what Polly would say if she made such a suggestion. There was nothing she could do except stick it out and cope as best she could, and learn now to accept the fact that Dee and Elizabeth would eventually be married.

She broached the subject to Polly across the kitchen table the next day. It was Christmas Eve, and she had come home early from the garage to help her prepare the Christmas dinner, and incidentally follow her uncle's practice of drawing all his cars off the road before lunchtime on Christmas Eve.

'I'm not risking my men or my cars on the road after twelve o'clock on that day,' he had declared years ago, when someone questioned why he chose to ground his fleet on what could have been one of the most profitable afternoons for the business of the whole winter season. 'There are still too many witless idiots who think they can have a party on the day they break up from work, and then jump into a car and drive home safely afterwards,' he growled savagely, still shaken after having his good paintwork scraped from stem to stern in a badly misjudged pass by a car driven by someone who had toasted the season too freely, partaking with the toasts more of over-confidence than common sense. Since then, Humphrey Manders had locked the gates of the garage at noon each Christmas Eve and gone home, giving Polly two pairs of willing hands to help with her preparations, he cheerfully keeping the fires stoked and ensuring that there were enough split logs to keep her happy over the holiday, and Sherry helping in the kitchen.

'Elizabeth will probably announce her engagement this Christmas,' Sherry told the housekeeper, blessing Polly's stern sense of propriety that she knew would forbid her asking who to. The thought of telling her it was Dee, and her possible reaction when he walked in, would be too much, she told herself. Polly could wait until she saw the announcement in the paper after the holiday, and she could not blame Sherry then for not saying anything before.

'She'll make a lovely bride.'

Polly's fingers slowed at their task, and her black eyes were unusually soft as they gazed into some far distance. What distance? And at whom? Sherry wondered. She often *had* wondered, about Polly. She was always known as Mrs. Flint, but that could, Sherry knew, be a complimentary title such as was often used by her generation in the Border country, when single women reached a certain age, and particularly if, like Polly, they were engaged in an activity like housekeeping. To Sherry's knowledge Polly had never mentioned a husband, and she had not seen any evidence about the house of a long-defunct Flint, such as a photograph, nor did she wear a wedding ring. Sherry wondered if some long-ago romance, however it had ended, would account for the housekeeper's avid interest in the weddings of anyone she knew.

Maybe when I'm like Polly I shall be just as interested, thought Sherry forlornly. She wouldn't marry at all unless she could marry Dee, and by the time she was as old as Polly the hurt of it would probably have lessened, although just now it seemed painful enough to last for a whole lifetime.

She pulled some more parsley under her knife and concentrated on her task of chopping it for the stuffing. It was springy stuff, difficult to chop, and her wrist ached. The sharp clack as the blade of her knife hit the board hammered like a pneumatic drill in her brain, until her head began to ache with slow, heavy throbs. She felt indifferent to the pain. It didn't agonize like heartache, she thought dully, and you couldn't take aspirin for that.

The rasp of a saw sounded harshly above the noise of her knife, then the familiar sound of thuds deeper than those she was making told her that Dee was following her uncle's example and, unasked, was splitting logs for the fires. Her heart twisted. This was what it would be like if we were married, she thought. Dee would cope with the outside chores, while she cooked for him in the kitchen. Only they wouldn't seem like chores then, if they were doing them for one another. She rubbed the back of her hand hastily across her eyes, and jumped when Polly spoke.

'What's the matter?'

The housekeeper's tone was sharp, as it always was, but Sherry was used to that and didn't mind. It was her eyes she was wary of, they were sharper than her tongue, and could see that which she desperately wished to hide.

'It's that onion I've just done for the bread sauce,' she lied hastily. 'It seemed to make the smell worse when I pricked it with the cloves.' Thank goodness what she said was partly true, the acrid smell hung in the kitchen as her witness, and it diverted Polly's too penetrating glance.

'Put it away from you, then.' Polly could always find a sensible remedy for everything. She picked up the offending orb and removed it and the breadcrumbs to a safer distance, and continued placidly to pick over the sprigs of thyme to add to Sherry's parsley.

'What colour will you be wearing?' She wanted as many details as possible, and Sherry roused herself to interest her.

'Pale coffee, I think. Elizabeth's dress will be cream lace, so if mine's a shade or two darker, with orange freesias, it should tone in well.'

'It will look good with your hair,' approved Polly, her eyes on Sherry's face. 'Unusual, too.'

'Anything would look good with Sherry's hair,' commented Dee gaily, appearing in the doorway with a huge armful of split logs. 'Mmmm, something smells good,' he sniffed appreciatively. 'Where do you want these, Polly?'

'Drop them in there.' Polly nodded towards the big hod that stood in a corner of the open hearth. 'If you'll keep that filled, they'll dry off nicely for the fires.' She accepted the fact that Dee would take his share of the jobs along with herself and Sherry. Normally such behaviour towards a guest would have scandalized the housekeeper, but she seemed to have accepted Dee as one of the household right from the start, thought Sherry. If it was she, and not Elizabeth, who was going to marry him, she would have had no qualms at all about Polly's reaction. The elderly woman seemed to lean on Dee, a thing that Sherry had never known her do with anyone else before, not even Humphrey Manders; on the one hand mothering him as if he was still a small boy, and on the other accepting his authority on a dozen minor matters with a curious mixture of strength and dependence that was outside even Sherry's knowledge of the woman who had raised her.

'It's gone warmer outside.' Dee dropped his armful into the hod with a rumble, and bent to pick up one or two stray logs that had escaped on to the hearth. The hod was full, so he put them behind the fire, and turned with his back to the hearth, spreading his hands out behind him to the quick flare of flame.

'It's going to snow,' Polly stated, kneeling to the oven to remove a tray of golden-looking mince pies. She tapped one with her knuckle experimentally, and satisfied, slid the tray onto the worktop next to her.

'I'll test it for you,' offered Dee with a wistful look in the direction of the tray, and Polly's lips twitched. Dee could take liberties with her that few would have dared, thought Sherry admiringly.

'Mind the currants, they'll be hot,' Polly warned, easing one out with the end of a knife and handing it across to him. 'And don't drop crumbs on my clean floor,' she added with a return to her usual asperity.

Sherry's eyes glinted at the momentary look of doubt that passed over his face, and his own met hers with a twinkle of fun as he hastily accepted the plate she slid in his direction across the table.

'I hope it doesn't snow for the carol service. It looks nice enough on a picture postcard,' she commented, 'but it can be a cold affair standing outside round a Christmas tree, particularly at the Castle Chapel. It catches all the wind from the downs up there. I suppose it's because it's against the town wall.'

'Are you going, Polly?' Dee cast a dubious eye out of the window.

'I'm staying here in the warm,' she refused, in a tone that brooked no argument. 'I've just told you, it's going to snow. My knee's been telling me so ever since I got up this morning.' She rose stiffly with another tray of mince pies.

'Let me stay and help.'

Sherry forgot her own troubles in instant sympathy. Polly's knee could be painfully disabling, and if she stayed behind Dee could take Elizabeth's present for her. The two friends always exchanged their gifts at the carol service on Christmas Eve, regarding the joyous, vocal get-together as the start of Christmas proper, as did half the town of whatever denomination they happened to be. If only Dee would go, and leave her behind with Polly, it would at least give her a few hours' respite from his company, and the hopeless yearning of her own wayward heart.

'Nonsense! You must go as usual. I can manage here quite well, there's only the clearing-up to do, and then I've finished.' Polly dashed her hopes. 'Make a cup of coffee and have a mince pie, and you'll do until dinner time.' With scrupulous fairness she handed Sherry one from the fresh batch.

'The first mince pie of the season. You ought to wish,' Dee reminded her.

'What about you?' she countered, using the saucepan of milk as an excuse to turn her head away. She had only one wish, and no mince pie could make that come true.

'I've already wished.' He did not enlarge, but Sherry had no difficulty in guessing his thoughts, and any wishes that he might have. Silently she sent a wish up as well, for their happiness, and for courage for herself. Maybe that was two wishes really, but they were so closely linked that she put them together and hoped desperately that they would both come true.

'You were right about the currants!' Dee told Polly ruefully, taking a hasty swallow of coffee. 'I'll run you

164

down to the carol-singing – that is if you'll have me?' he offered Sherry. He seemed to be in high good humour, and she nodded numbly, unable to speak, using her own mouthful of pastry as a poor excuse for silence.

If she would have him! To have and to hold until ... No, don't think about it. She pushed the rest of her drink away, unable to swallow any more, and fled for the door.

'I'll go and get Elizabeth's present. Shan't be long,' she called behind her, and ran up the stairs to her room, blinking to clear her misted vision. She heard Dee start up the stairs behind her, probably to get his overcoat, but she did not wait for him. Dared not wait, for fear he should see her tears and guess her secret. Refusing to look round, she stumbled blindly into her room and thudded the door to behind her, leaning against the stout wood with her eyes closed, longing to remain in its sanctuary, but knowing that she must not. She heard the squeak of Dee's wardrobe door in the next room. She would have to hurry, or he would wonder what was keeping her. She reached inside her own closet and grabbed the first thing that came to hand, the same trouser suit she had worn on her first visit to the plantation. The woolly cap and mitts were still in the pocket, and she pulled them on, swinging the scarf round her throat. Elizabeth's present lay on her dressing table, ready wrapped in scarlet paper with a gay ribbon bow finishing off the top. She scooped it up and hastened back downstairs before her courage failed her. Dee was waiting for her in the hall. He had a parcel in his hand, presumably for Elizabeth, but it was equally as square as hers, so it could not be the ring. Perhaps he intended to keep that until Christmas Day, and give it to her then. It was the traditional time for the weaving of such a knot, just as Easter was for its final tying. A sudden thought struck her.

'Will you be in for Christmas dinner tomorrow?' He hadn't mentioned that he would be out, though of course he might have done to Polly.

'Yes, I hadn't thought of going out at all. That is, if I'm not in the way?' His voice sounded hesitant.

'Of course not. I was thinking of meals, that's all,' she assured him, hiding her surprise. Perhaps Elizabeth had thought that she and Polly would be lonely on Christmas Day without Humphrey Manders, and had forgone Dee's company for their sake. It would be typically thoughtful of her, thought Sherry, though she wished her friend had been more selfishly inclined on this occasion, the day would have been easier for her to get through without Dee's company. She was already beginning to feel the strain of hiding her feelings from Polly, let alone from Dee himself.

'We're here!'

She turned to find him watching her, with an odd expression on his face, his vivid eyes searching hers with disconcerting keenness, as if he would read the thoughts that lay behind them.

'Still thinking about meals?'

'Polly's cooking is worth thinking about,' she parried lightly, returning to the present with a rush. Lost in thought, she had not seen the brightly lit Christmas tree staked out on the lawns surrounding the chapel, nor the cheerful crowds that, muffled against the weather, thronged the frozen grass, waiting for the white-robed choir to appear, in the meantime happy to stand about in groups and talk as friend met friend and took the opportunity of exchanging gifts with those they would not see again until after the festival was over.

'Elizabeth's somewhere about, there's her car along by the wall.' Dee scanned the crowd about them. 'There she is, and it looks as if she's brought Andy with her.'

'He wanted to join in a bit of British tradition,' laughed Elizabeth, arriving at their side breathless and dishevelled, 'so I brought him along.'

Sherry felt her spirits lift with relief, and immediately dropped her plan to lose herself in the crowd and leave Elizabeth and Dee on their own. With the Canadian there, she would not feel quite such an interloper. His easygoing friendliness was a balm to her sorely tried spirits, and she silently thanked whatever wind of fortune had brought him to the Lomax works, and stranded him there over the holiday.

'Happy Christmas!' she cried, and handed her parcel to Elizabeth, who promptly handed her one back with a warning.

'Don't open it until tomorrow.'

'I'll make sure she doesn't.' Before Sherry realized what he was going to do, Dee calmly relieved her of her parcel and tucked it under his arm, looking down from his superior height at her disappointed 'Oh!' 'It'll be in your stocking tomorrow morning,' he promised. 'I'm deputy Santa this year,' he explained to Andy, who winked broadly and, putting out a large hand, wrapped it round the parcel Sherry had just given to Elizabeth.

'Thief!' Elizabeth grasped at it too late.

'Just to be on the safe side,' said the Canadian blandly, tucking it under his mac.

'Put this one with it.' Dee handed his own parcel

over. 'You can give them both to her after breakfast tomorrow morning.'

So he really didn't intend to see Elizabeth on Christmas Day. They would all be together at the children's party on Boxing Day, of course, but remembering previous years Sherry doubted if there would be any quiet moments long enough, let alone private enough, for such an intimate occasion as a betrothal.

A burst of singing interrupted her thoughts, and a magpie stream of black-and-white robed choirboys paced slowly through the chapel doors towards the brilliantly lit tree. The deep, pealing tones of an organ, muted by the walls of the chapel, accompanied their voices in a ringing backcloth of sound, and Sherry gazed at the young, angelic faces upturned with childish wonder towards the decorative glitter that reflected in their shining eyes. She smiled. They would all be at the party the day after tomorrow, and she had no doubt that their expressions then would be less angelic, as would their well-scrubbed appearance after an hour or two's mixture of party fare and boisterous games.

'Let's hold on to one another, or we'll get separated in this crush,' gasped Elizabeth, grabbing at Sherry for support as the crowd backed to make room for the file of choristers. She put her arm about Sherry's waist, and Dee did the same, their hands linking behind her back and pressing against her in a hold that seemed to burn through her jacket. She was completely dwarfed by the other three, and the Canadian shot her an amused look.

'Hold on to whatever you can reach,' he smiled, needless advice since Dee had a firm grasp of her with his other hand, and did not seem in any hurry to let her go even when the crowd came to a standstill and settled down as the organ inside the chapel softly started on the strains of another carol.

The sound was echoed from the black-and-white circle surrounding the tree, their young voices rising high and clear into the winter darkness, carrying on a tradition that had begun when the Border wars ended, and people could foregather in safety for the first time in centuries, and make the rolling green hills echo to the sound of their singing that had for too long echoed to the cries of battle.

Sherry relaxed in the shelter of Dee's arm, imprinting the scene on her mind. There would never be another Christmas when his arm would shelter her from the winter cold. It was a cold that she felt would remain in her heart whatever the season, for the rest of her days, as long as the memory would have to last her, sharp and clear, in a way that no amount of time could dim.

'You're not singing.'

She hadn't realized that she was silent until Dee spoke, his face concerned as he looked down at her, and she smiled up at him.

'I'll join in the next one, it's not so high.'

She would join in, and be happy, for this one night, to make her memory a warm one, so that when, like Polly, she gazed back at it across the distance of years, she could feel glad that it had once been there.

For an hour the choir sang, and the crowd sang with them, the music rolling out across the downs, echoing back from the dark plantation, resounding from the frozen water of Battle Pools, until the encircling town walls rang with echoes, and even Sherry's heart lifted into a forgetfulness that she would fain have held to her when it ended. At last it was over, and a great quiet descended on the crowd as they received the words of the ancient blessing before the choir started to life again, circling the tree once, and then filing through the now quiet spectators until the doors of the chapel received them, and their voices became muted like the organ, and slowly died away.

Sherry sighed.

Her mind and heart felt strangely drained of feeling. If only it would last, she thought hopelessly, but she knew that it could not. That the respite was only a temporary one, and she had to accept the hurt as part of the memory, as the shadow that is always cast by sunlight, the brightest rays throwing the darkest shade.

A robed arm reached upwards to a switchbox in the chapel entrance, and one by one the lights of the tree dimmed and went out, leaving a pool of empty blackness that so short a time before had been peopled by laughter and light. And as if it had waited for the darkness as a signal, very gently it began to snow.

CHAPTER TWELVE

ELIZABETH's parcel was at the foot of Sherry's bed the next morning. She could feel it with the tip of her big toe when she stretched to hazy consciousness, to the sound of a spoon tinkling in a saucer.

'It was my turn to get the tea this morning, Polly,' she murmured sleepily, struggling upright in bed and rubbing a hand across eyes still dazed from slumber. 'You must rest,' she remembered drowsily.

'It isn't Polly, and I don't need a rest,' retorted a masculine voice from above her head. 'Happy Christmas!' Dee's hand descended on her hair and ruffled her curls into even wilder disorder. 'Drink your tea before it gets cold,' he commanded, and then he was gone, closing her door quietly behind him before she could find her voice.

Sherry heard his steps go along the landing to Polly's room, his knuckles rap sharply on her door to make sure she was awake before he took her tea in, and then the housekeeper's voice responding in a pleased tone to his cheerful greeting.

She fought down a quick, choking feeling aroused by the thought of her uncle's absence, and reached for her cup. The tea was hot and sweet and brought her to full wakefulness, and a saner sense of relief that Humphrey Manders was making such good progress. Happier on that count at least, she reached for her presents. Elizabeth's was first, and she chuckled as she surveyed the dainty white underwear reposing in the gift box. They had both had the same idea, only the replica she had given to her friend had been in Elizabeth's favourite primrose-yellow. Sherry wondered, achingly, if she would use it as part of her trousseau.

Refusing to allow her thoughts in that direction further rein, she untied the bow of her next parcel. It was flat, with a bump in the middle that roused her curiosity. She carefully parted the mass of tissue paper in which the flatness rested, and gasped as her own face stared back at her. Mounted in a plain wooden frame to match the picture that Dee had given to her on the day of the storm – it seemed years ago now – was a beautifully executed pen-and-ink sketch of herself, done against a background of the fir plantation, her face depicted in clear, sensitive lines of skilful penmanship that caught her breath in her throat.

Was this how Dee saw her? This carefree, laughing picture of a girl with wind-tumbled hair, standing on a steep hill slope among forest trees, her arms joyously outstretched as if to embrace the spread of the meres at her feet, and the wild, flighting geese that rose on powerful wings towards the empty sky. This sort of country was Dee's choice, she knew, the rugged wilderness to which he came as often as he had a moment to spare. It would be hers too, she thought wistfully, if she was by his side.

A hard point digging into the centre of her palm made her realize she was clutching the lumpy something wrapped in bright paper that stood in the middle of the picture frame, and she undid the rustling folds, revealing a miniature china figurine of a jenny wren. Its tiny head, cocked to one side, regarded her with pert inquiry, and brought a quick, answering smile to her lips. She drew her legs up under the bedclothes and put her new acquisition on the top of the resulting mound, hugging her knees delightedly, so that she and the jenny wren were looking at one another eye to eye. The colour of the fine china was superbly natural, as was the stance of the bird, so lifelike that Sherry almost expected to hear its loud trill that Dee had identified for her when they were in the scrub oak spinney.

'You can thank me properly tomorrow, at the party,' he murmured teasingly when she ran downstairs to thank him. He was proudly displaying his tie-clip to Polly from where it held the new tie that Sherry knew the housekeeper had bought for him.

'I'm glad you like your wren.' Suddenly, he bent forward and kissed her lightly on the forehead, indicating as his excuse the mistletoe that he had tacked up on a beam in the hall. Sherry had not seen him put it up. She had left it on the hall stand when they came in together the day it had been gathered, and so far as she knew it was still there. He saluted Polly in the same way, a liberty few would have dared take, thought Sherry, but the housekeeper made no objection, and carried on showing Sherry the black suede gloves that Dee had presented her with along with her early cup of tea, only protesting when they firmly ushered her into the dining-room. There was already a good fire burning in the grate. Dee must have seen to that as well, thought Sherry gratefully.

'You sit and rest your knee,' she insisted. 'You know I always bring you your breakfast on Christmas morning.'

Having settled Polly she hurried to the kitchen to start the breakfast. She did not expect Dee to help her, he had already done quite enough anyhow, she thought, grateful for the warmth that glowed from the range when she opened the door, but he was right behind her when she reached the stove, and he started to work along with her with the ease of someone accustomed to coping for himself.

'I live in a bachelor flat,' he answered her look of surprise. 'It's either learn how, or eat out of tins,' he added ruefully, turning the tap into the kettle.

Sherry cracked eggs into a saucepan and reached for the seasoning. She had almost forgotten Dee's flat. She and Polly had got used to having him around the house, and they would both miss him when he left, she thought with a pang, whipping the contents of her pot with more vigour than was necessary.

'Look out! You'll have a burnt offering on your hands,' Dee cried, reaching out a hurried arm and grabbing the toast from beneath the grill. He waved it to and fro until the flames subsided, and sorted out some more bread. 'The tea's ready. I'll take it in and do these with the toasting-fork in front of the dining-room fire. It's bright enough by now.'

'You must have got up horribly early.' Sherry felt guilty. It should have been she who was looking after him. 'Leave the burnt ones on the table, I'll throw them out for the birds later on.' She pulled back the curtains, and the hard, bright light that greeted her from the whitened garden was evidence enough of what had happened during the night. Dee followed her glance.

'I'll sweep the paths clear for you after breakfast,' he offered. 'It'll give me an appetite for that turkey you're cooking. It smells good already.'

Sherry had set the cooker for the early hours of the morning, and the bird had been heating gently through, filling the kitchen with a rich, appetizing scent.

'I can come out and help you. There'll be nothing to do in here until we have to put the vegetables on just before dinner.'

Sweeping snow would help her to pass the morning, and give her something to occupy her mind, as well as tire her so that she slept when she went to bed. Suddenly sleep, and the forgetfulness it brought, had become important. She picked up the burnt toast when she went outside after breakfast, and a handful of crusts left over from when she made the breadcrumbs for the stuffing the day before.

'I wish I'd got my camera with me,' remarked Dee, watching the continual flutter about her feet as a flock of birds, starved into fearlessness by the hard weather, swooped to the feast, the smaller varieties coming right to her feet as some protection from the bullying of the larger, stronger ones.

'There don't seem to be any wrens?'

'It's very rare for them to feed from household scraps,' Dee said regretfully. 'That's why so many of them die in a very hard winter. They'll be up in the thickets, creeping among the undergrowth where the snow can't reach, and finding what food they can there.'

'If only they wouldn't gobble it all at once. There's nothing left for the latecomers,' mourned Sherry.

'You can easily remedy that,' he retorted. 'Drive some nails in a few of the fence posts, and spear a loaf of bread on them. They can help themselves then whenever they feel like it.'

'Let's do it now. Polly's got a couple of loaves to spare, I know, the baker duplicated her order by mistake.' The sight of half-a-dozen sparrows hopelessly scratching the snow drove Sherry into action. 'Uncle

Humph has got some nails in the potting shed.'

She hurried indoors and came out with two large loaves tucked under her arm.

'You hold on to those and I'll get the nails for you.' Dee rummaged about among the boxes in the shed, and emerged triumphant with a handful of long ones, and a hammer. 'Let's drive one of these into each post. If we put them where they can be seen from the windows you'll be able to enjoy watching the feast.' He accepted her interest with the enthusiasm of the dedicated, and soon the frost-sharpened air rang with hammer blows as he drove the nails in with sure, hard strokes.

'There are only the two loaves.' Sherry sounded doubtful. 'I don't know if Polly will spare any more bread, the baker doesn't come until Thursday.'

'Two of that size will be plenty for now. Break them in half. Here, let me,' as she fumbled with the large tin loaves, their tough crust resisting her mittened fingers. Swiftly, he split them both in two. 'That allows the little birds to get at the soft part more easily, until the dampness has taken the toughness from the crust,' he explained. 'These two will fill four posts, and you can renew them when they're finished. Brown bread's better,' he acknowledged, 'but I don't suppose they'll quibble with the weather this hard.' He ducked back inside the shed and replaced his tool with a stiff brush. 'Now for the paths. Come and help, you look frozen standing there.'

The bitter air drew their breaths in grey clouds about them, and Sherry hastily equipped herself, taking the path parallel to Dee, and sweeping as hard as she could to keep in time with him across the other side of the lawn. Soon her cheeks were hot and she stopped for breath. He looked back at her and laughed.

'That's warmed you up,' he approved. 'If you put a bit of energy into it you might even catch me up,' he teased.

Quick as thought Sherry retaliated. Bending swiftly, she scooped up a handful of snow. It was crisp enough to ball nicely, and with surprisingly accurate aim she threw it at Dee's head. He ducked out of the way and came upright again in time to meet her next missile fair and square on his coat sleeve. He laughed, and lobbed one back, and in seconds a volley of hastily rolled snowballs crossed and recrossed the lawn. Sherry gave no quarter, and asked none, and soon they were both spattered from head to foot with snow.

'Pax!' He lifted his broom aloft, and Sherry chuckled helplessly as his white handkerchief fluttered from the top. 'We're getting soaked. Let me brush you down.' He performed a quick but thorough valeting, and ended by plucking off her knitted cap. 'Shake this clear, it's all in the bobble on the top.' While she complied he brushed himself down and took her broom from her. 'Polly's signalling, it looks as if she might have a cup of coffee ready. You go in, and I'll put these away.'

He strode off towards the shed, and later accepted the towel that Polly thrust into his hands to rub his hair dry as he came into the kitchen. 'The stove will dry the rest off.' He finished his mince pie and reached for another.

'Don't spoil your dinner,' Polly warned, and he shook his head emphatically.

'Don't worry, I won't.'

'He's going to need his dinner,' prophesied Sherry darkly. 'With all that there is to do this afternoon ...'

'I'll help wash up.' His offer was immediate.

'I mean after that,' she told him. 'You said you'd help decorate the cars tomorrow, right?' He nodded. 'We always pump up the balloons on Christmas afternoon, there's no time to do them on Boxing Day, and it needs about sixteen balloons to a car. There are five cars going,' she informed him, and her lips wrinkled at his startled look. 'Oh, we've got a balloon pump, we don't blow them up with our mouths,' she assured him. 'Just the same, there's a lot of balloons, and they all have to be tied, with a bit of string left for fixing them to the car. Any that are over we let loose at the party, it gets things going.'

'Let me do the tying,' he insisted after the third balloon on which he had expended energy had begun to look sad. 'Your strings are allowing them to leak. Girls are hopeless at tying knots,' he grumbled, and Sherry flinched inwardly.

Not the kind of knots that mattered, she thought, her earlier high spirits deflating as quickly as the balloons. Those sort of knots lasted a lifetime. Numbly she handed over her bag of cut strings, taking the pump from his hands in turn, and after that the job went more smoothly until the room seemed filled with brightly coloured spheres and sausage shapes.

'We'll have to net them, or we'll never get them in the van tomorrow morning.'

Even in the nets, they only just managed to close the van doors the next morning on the gay assembly, and Sherry's hands hovered over her ears, anticipating a succession of loud pops as Dee slammed them shut.

'They're intact – I think,' he grinned, and gave her a boost up into the high seat. The Christmas roads were deserted by their normal traffic, but the journey took them longer than usual as Dee checked his speed after a sledge with two laughing children aboard whizzed in front of him without any warning out of a side road. The streets were alive with happy youngsters, intent on enjoying the snow while it lasted, and the hilly nature of the district made it a paradise for those who could secure anything flat that they could sit on and slide.

'There'll be a few in bandages by this afternoon,' Dee prophesied, and Sherry laughed.

'I don't suppose it will affect their appetites. They'll be as hungry as hunters after a morning playing outside.'

'That's a point,' he conceded. 'If you don't mind I think I'll leave you to decorate the cars and take the bigger van with me. They just might want an extra lot of food taken in, and it's best to be on the safe side.'

Sherry wished, longingly, that he would stay with her, grasping the nettle of the pain it would cause in the knowledge that she had a whole lifetime ahead to try and find the balm, if one existed, for the stings. After today it would never be the same, every moment was a precious stone in the necklet of hours, and once the remorseless clock had joined the clasp in a complete circle there would never be room again to add another bead.

'I've got something special for your car, miss. Come and see.'

Paul hurried to her side as she quit the van, urging her into the garage, obviously longing to undo the back of the vehicle and release the balloons and decorations into the eager hands of the drivers, each intent on vying with the others to make his car the gayest in the cavalcade. Sherry thrust her thoughts away and gave him the van key. It was selfish to let her own unhappiness intrude on such a day and spoil the others' enjoyment as well as her own. Pretending an interest she did not feel, she peered over the young apprentice's shoulder, and her misery turned to consternation as he dragged a spiky apparition from the front seat of her car, and held it up proudly for her to view. The last time she had seen that particular stag's head it had been in the hall of Ben's house, plentifully draped with the family's hats and scarves.

'Oh, Paul! Does Ben know?' she asked nervously.

'Oh yes, miss. He let me have it.' Sherry heaved a sigh of relief. 'He took a lot of persuading,' he went on, shattering her momentary peace of mind, 'but he gave way in the end. If it snows,' he added with ghoulish interest, 'It'll probably finish Rudolf off.'

It probably would, thought Sherry, regarding the moth-eaten ancient with dismay.

'Look, I've got a Father Christmas to drive him.' He displayed an inflated rubber Santa Claus, complete with long, cotton wool beard. 'I thought I would fix them to the roof rack of your car, with some ribbons from the Santa Claus on to the tips of the deer's antlers. If we put a net of balloons for his sack of toys, you'll be able to lead the rest of the cars in style.'

His enthusiasm was infectious, and Sherry felt her spirits lifting so that she even joined in the cheerful banter that passed between the men working on the other cars, and felt a glow of pride when she surveyed the assembled parade.

'It's the best we've done yet,' commented Syd. 'A pity the gaffer can't see it.'

'We'll send him a picture.' Dee appeared through

the gate, swinging a camera, and laughing at their imaginative display. 'I thought your uncle might like to see what you'd done,' he said. 'Line up, and we'll send him a snap with all of you on it.'

The clear snow light was excellent for his purpose, and he took several snaps from different angles when Syd intervened.

'Let's have one with you and Mr. Lawrence on it, miss,' he suggested. 'You're in this with us,' he reminded Dee, 'even if your van isn't decorated like the cars.'

'Suits me.' Dee flung cheerful arms about Sherry, and lifted her on to the bonnet of her car. 'Perch up there, where you can be seen,' he told her, retaining his hold so that she should not slip on her precarious seat. His arm felt warm and strong about her, and his smile was cheerful as befitted their background. She forced her own smile to match. The photograph would be an addition to her memories, and cameras did not lie. Fear of what the snap might reveal of her feelings polished the brightness of her expression, and then they were sat round the radiator in the garage, eating into the hamper of turkey sandwiches and mince pies that Polly had sent for them all, and she could check the flow of her thoughts by keeping her hands busy making coffee for the men, hiding the fact that she herself was not eating, except to Dee's observant eyes.

'Sit down and have yours, now. Paul will do the rest.'

It took a mug of coffee with each sandwich to enable her to swallow the food, but somehow she managed it, parrying Dee's concerned question.

'I'm all right, it's the excitement, that's all.'

She thrust the empty wrappers back into the

hamper, slid the last mince pie into Paul's willing fingers, and ducked into the driving seat of her car.

'See you at the party,' she called to Dee, reluctant to meet his probing glance, and with a wave and a smile which she hoped would deceive him she started the engine into life and led the line of cars out of the gates, thankful to let her mind embrace the task before her, and leave her, if only for a few short hours, in what passed for peace.

Her whole attention was soon taken by successive loads of excited children, and the cars scurried to and fro like ants across the town collecting all those who had no other means of getting to the party.

'To think we've got to take all that lot back afterwards!' groaned one of the drivers, surveying the noisily successful gathering with pretended gloom.

'Some of them will probably be feeling sick by then,' expected Sherry resignedly, sternly refusing one small boy a fourth helping of jelly. 'Try a piece of bread and butter for a change,' she suggested. His expression left her in no doubt what he thought of bread and butter at a party, and Elizabeth chuckled.

'I don't know where the time's gone to,' she complained, flopping exhaustedly into a chair. 'Where's Dee?'

'Somewhere in the scrum, I imagine.' Sherry hadn't caught more than a fleeting glimpse of him all the afternoon, they were both kept too busy coping with the lively guests to have any time for grown-ups, though she had imagined he would be alongside Elizabeth.

'Andy's immersed, too,' her friend said unsympathetically. 'But it'll quieten down in a few minutes. Dad's playing Father Christmas as usual, and they'll soon forget their games for a bit while he hands out the presents.'

Sherry had forgotten the comparative calm that followed the present giving. Maybe that was when Dee would give Elizabeth the ring, she thought. It was the one quiet time during the afternoon when they would be able to snatch a moment to themselves. The sound of sleigh bells cut across the loud buzz of noise in the canteen, coming, Sherry knew, from a carefully concealed gramophone in one of the kitchens, and an expectant hush settled on the children, to be broken by awe-struck 'oohs' as the main doors flew open, revealing Hereward Lomax, efficiently disguised in a long red cloak, and realistically bent under a mountainous sack that she knew was mostly filled with even more balloons – the presents were tactfully disguised in a grotto of coloured paper at the base of the brightly lit tree. He paused, gazed at the assembled throng that gazed just as earnestly back at him, and smiled.

'Hello, children!'

His deep, ringing voice brought an eager response, and in seconds he had achieved the impossible. Each child was sat quietly on the floor, the little ones nearest to him, in a huge semi-circle of expectancy. He stooped, reaching behind his sack, and picked up a gaily wrapped parcel, and read the name on it aloud. Soon he had a stream of children trotting up to him, each one receiving their individual gift, and a murmur of 'oohs' and 'aahs' accompanied the rustle of paper as small fingers tasted the pleasure of unwrapping their particular surprise. One small girl brought a ripple of laughter from the older ones by insisting on kissing the donor.

'I wonder if I should have the same luck?' inquired

Dee, of nobody in particular, from the shadows behind them. The lights at the back of the hall had been dimmed, leaving only the brilliant circle about the tree.

'Why not try it and see?' suggested a Canadian voice interestedly.

'I'll bet she's got a jammy face,' chuckled Elizabeth.

'Have you been eating jam?'

Dee was behind Sherry, raising her from her chair, his fingers under her chin so that she was forced to look up at him. Taken off guard, she had no time to mask the expression in her eyes that the unexpected sound of his voice had aroused.

'I said you could thank me properly for the jenny wren when we were at the party.' He pointed to the large bunch of mistletoe hung above their heads. The bride's bunch. Hers had been for the bridesmaid – or the best man. He bent his head above her, and Sherry's trembling limbs were powerless to pull away, just as she was powerless to stop her own joyous response as his lips met hers. He drew away from her at last, his eyes dark with an expression that she felt too distressed to read. He must know, now. He could not help but know that she loved him, her own kiss had betrayed her. Sick at heart, she leaned against him, momentarily relying on the support of the one arm he kept about her, while his other fumbled in his pocket. It came out holding a small box, and he flicked the top off with his thumb.

'If I give you another present, will you kiss me like that again?'

'Don't tease, Dee. I can't bear it!' The cry stayed inside her, her lips too stiff to form the words, and her throat ached too much to allow her to use her voice.

Faintly, she felt him fumble for her hand, felt something round and smooth slide on to her finger. She looked down, her wet eyes blurring the glittering facets of light from the sparkling circle of stones about her finger.

'It's an – eternity ring?' Her voice came in a whisper.

'That's how I think of marriage.' His voice was soft now, all the teasing done. 'For better, for worse, till death us do part.'

'Our view exactly.' Andy's voice came crisply out of the shadows, and Sherry turned and saw that he had his arm around Elizabeth. She did not seem to mind, in fact seemed quite at home there, and when she spoke her voice was merry.

'I told you the chief bridesmaid always marries the best man, and you didn't believe me,' she accused Sherry. 'Dee's promised to be best man to Andy. He popped the question yesterday,' she confided, 'and I've been dying to tell you ever since, but we don't seem to have had a minute to ourselves all afternoon. Oh, I haven't got my ring yet,' she said, seeing Sherry glance at her hand, 'we're going to announce it officially in the New Year, but this afternoon Andy asked Dee if he would do the honours for him. It's too far for Andy's brother to come all the way from Canada for the wedding, and we want it to be soon so that I can go back with him when his business trip is over.' She turned to Dee. 'You said you'd got half of Sherry's present. Was that the ring?' she asked.

'The one half was the ring,' allowed Dee promptly. 'The other half – the important one – was knowing whether Sherry would accept it. And I do know – don't I?' His voice was only slightly hesitant.

Sherry nodded speechlessly. He did not need to ask her. Her kiss had told him, and now her eyes put the seal on what it had said. He gathered her close, and this time she did not attempt to draw away.

'I'll help you to look for your house,' she offered eventually, in a rather breathless voice that held a note of laughter.

'Our house,' he corrected. 'Between us, we'll make it a home.' There was a world of contentment in his voice as he said the word 'home'.

'Tell me something?' Her voice was a quiet murmur from about the level of his heart. 'Why did you say the picture of the jenny wren suited me best?' Her curiosity got the better of her, and she had to know.

She felt a tremor of amusement run through him, and then his voice, deep and quiet, and for her ear alone.

'Because the wrens are little, and plucky, and they make wonderful partners for one another,' he whispered. 'And of all the birds, they're my very favourite,' he assured her.

OMNIBUS — The 3-in-1 HARLEQUIN
only $1.75 per volume

Here is a great new exciting idea from Harlequin. THREE GREAT ROMANCES — complete and unabridged — BY THE SAME AUTHOR — in one deluxe paperback volume — for the unbelievably low price of only $1.75 per volume.

We have chosen some of the finest works of four world-famous authors . . .

> CATHERINE AIRLIE
>
> VIOLET WINSPEAR ②
>
> KATHRYN BLAIR
>
> ROSALIND BRETT

. . . and reprinted them in the 3-in-1 Omnibus. Almost 600 pages of pure entertainment for just $1.75 each. A TRULY "JUMBO" READ!

These four Harlequin Omnibus volumes are now available. The following pages list the exciting novels by each author.

Climb aboard the Harlequin Omnibus now! The coupon below is provided for your convenience in ordering.

Catherine Airlie

Omnibus

This author's fine books have become famous throughout North America, and are greatly anticipated by readers of romance all over the world. The three stories chosen for this volume highlight her unusual talent of combining the elements of compassion and suspense in one exceptional novel.

. . . . CONTAINING:

DOCTOR OVERBOARD . . . on board a luxury liner, cruising between the Canary Islands, Trinidad and Barbados, a young Scot, Mairi Finlay, is facing a traumatic experience, torn between her growing affection for the young ship's surgeon, and her duty to her employer who has set her an impossible task . . . (#979).

NOBODY'S CHILD . . . from London England, we are taken to a medieval castle, the Schloss Lamberg, situated on the outskirts of the City of Vienna, to brush shoulders with the aristocracy of the music world. Amidst all of this beauty, a young girl, Christine Dainton, is submerged in the romance of a lifetime with one of the most admired men in the world . . . (#1258).

A WIND SIGHING . . . Jean Lorimer's life has always been happy here, on the small Hebridean Island of Kinnail, owned by the Lorimer family for centuries. Now, Jean and her mother are grief stricken on the death of her father. They will surely lose their home too, for Kinnail was always inherited by the eldest male in the family, whose arrival they expect any day now (#1328).

$1.75 per volume

Violet Winspear ②

Omnibus

Only once in a very long time, does an author such as Violet Winspear emerge from the hosts of writers of popular novels. Her effortless portrayal of the human emotions experienced in romantic conflict has contributed greatly to her acknowledgement as one of the finest writers of romance in the world.

. . . . CONTAINING:

BRIDE'S DILEMMA . . . on the beautiful island of Ste. Monique, young Tina Manson fought hard to preserve her newfound happiness in a blissful marriage to the man she had loved since their very first meeting. But there was someone else who loved him, and whose endless scheming proved powerful enough to crush Tina's world . . . (#1008).

TENDER IS THE TYRANT . . . Lauri Garner, almost eighteen years old, had such an alarming innocence about her. She had been dancing with the great di Corte Ballet Company only a short time when she fell in love with Signor di Corte. Unknown to Lauri, he sought only to mould her into another Prima Donna Travilla—no matter what the cost . . . (#1208).

THE DANGEROUS DELIGHT . . . it would take a few hours before the coach could proceed. Faye was grateful for the break in her journey from Lisbon, and the chance of a short walk. To be discovered as a trespasser on the grounds of the estate of none other than the Conde Vincente de Rebelo Falcao was an innocent crime—the consequences of which were most serious . . . (#1344).

$1.75 per volume

Kathryn Blair

Omnibus

Kathryn Blair's outstanding work has become famous and most appreciated by those who seek real-life characters against backgrounds which create and hold the interest throughout the entire story, thus producing the most captivating and memorable romantic novels available today.

. . . . CONTAINING:

DOCTOR WESTLAND . . . Tess Carlen is invited to recuperate in Tangier after suffering almost fatal injuries in an accident. On the voyage, Tess agrees to look after a small boy, and to deliver him to his father on arrival. By doing so, Tess becomes deeply embroiled in the mystery of Tangier which cloaks Dr. Philip Westland and his young son . . . (#954).

BATTLE OF LOVE . . . on the death of her husband, Catherine and her small son are offered a home by her father-in-law, Leon Verender, co-guardian of the boy. Chaos develops rapidly between them, caused by conflicting ideas on how to raise a child. Leon's scheming fiancée then delivers an ultimatum to Catherine—making life for her and her son impossible . . . (#1038).

FLOWERING WILDERNESS . . . a rubber plantation in Africa was no place for a woman as far as David Raynor was concerned. Nicky Graham had a great deal of courage, and she was determined to stay. Alas, before long, Nicky was forced to leave, but now she was very much in love with the same David Raynor . . . (#1148).

$1.75 per volume

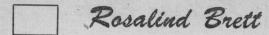

Rosalind Brett

Omnibus

A writer with an excitingly different appeal that transports the reader on a journey of enchantment to far-off places where warm, human people live in true to life circumstances, Miss Brett's refreshing touch to the age-old story of love, continues to fascinate her ever-increasing number of faithful readers.

. . . . CONTAINING:

THE GIRL AT WHITE DRIFT . . . Jerry Lake had travelled from England to Canada to live with her unknown guardian, Dave Farren. On arrival, Mr. Farren drove Jerry to his home, White Drift Farm, explaining that a few months' farm life would strengthen and build a fine body. To her utter horror, Jerry realized that this man thought she was a boy! . . . (#1101).

WINDS OF ENCHANTMENT . . . in Kanos, Africa, in surroundings of intense heat, oppressive jungle, insects and fever, Pat Brading faces the heartbreak of losing her father. The acute depression and shock she suffers in the following months gradually subside, and slowly she becomes aware that she is now married to a man who revolts her and whom she must somehow, escape . . . (#1176).

BRITTLE BONDAGE . . . when Venetia wrote the letter which had brought Blake Garrard immediately to her side in a time of need, she had felt great sorrow and bewilderment. Now, some time and a great deal of pain later, it was the contents of another letter which must drive her away from him. Only now, Blake was her husband . . . (#1319).

$1.75 per volume